JEFFERSON DAVIS

BEFORE HE WORE CONFEDERATE GRAY

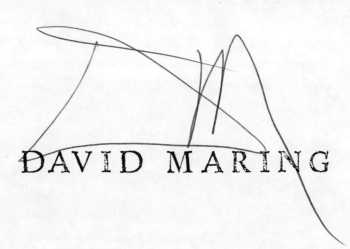

DAVID MARING

THIS BOOK, JEFFERSON DAVIS BEFORE HE WORE CONFEDERATE GRAY, IS A WORK OF FICTION. All characters, names, incidents, organizations, and dialogue in this novel are either the products of the author's imagination or are used fictitiously. However, it is written within a historical framework, and therefore certain characters, places, events, and groups are based on research of a particular era.

ISBN: 1494493314
ISBN 13: 9781494493318

Library of Congress Control Number: 2013923016
CreateSpace Independent Publishing Platform
North Charleston, South Carolina

FOREWORD

Jefferson Davis was born into a society created by the revolution and by the expansion of territory following American independence. His father had fought against the British invaders in South Carolina and Georgia, and two brothers had fought at the Battle of New Orleans. When he was ten years old, Jeff spent weeks with Andrew Jackson on his plantation. This background played an important role in forming his political views on what constituted the correct role of Washington in dealing with the States. But the greatest influence on his philosophy of government was by his oldest brother.

Joseph was twenty-three years old when Jeff was born. After the death of their father, he assumed the role of a father figure and provided Jeff with the resources necessary to become a distinguished public servant.

Before his election as President of the Confederacy, Jeff had graduated from West Point, served as an officer in the Army on the Indian frontier, and fought under Zachary Taylor during the Mexican War. His political life included service in the House of Representatives, the Senate, and a term as Secretary of War during the Pierce administration.

THE EARLY
YEARS

After Jefferson Davis finished packing, he sat by the window and looked out at the bluegrass that covered the school grounds of Saint Thomas in Springfield where he had spent the last two years. It had been quite an adjustment for him to be separated from his family. When he first arrived, he cried quietly during the night so the others boys would not hear him. Although Jeff missed his family, he had been treated well by the priests. He was somewhat of a curiosity, as the only Protestant in the student body. Except for the usual beating that all boys received for failure to learn, Jeff was content with his environment. He admired the priests. If they had encouraged him, he would not have resisted conversion to their faith. But Father Tuite had guided him away from becoming a Catholic for reasons that Jeff would never understand. This early experience left him always prejudiced in their favor, although he was surrounded by bias against Catholics after he left the school.

As Jeff boarded the steamboat, *Aetna,* at Louisville, he was greeted by Charles Green, his guardian during his stay at Saint Thomas. He would be responsible for Jeff until they reached Natchez where a brother, Isaac, would be waiting to take him home to Rosemont Plantation.

Charles had accepted the responsibility for Jeff when he met the boy's father, Samuel, at a gathering in Woodville. The man had approached him after he learned that Charles was about to depart for Springfield, Kentucky to study law. Samuel had obtained a commitment from him to keep in contact with his son. During the last two years he had visited the school frequently to meet with the headmaster and corresponded with Samuel to report on Jeff's progress.

The hour was late when the *Aetna* arrived in Natchez. Isaac called out Jeff's name as his brother stepped off the gangplank onto the wharf. At first, Jeff did not recognize Isaac. Two years had brought about a change in his physical appearance. A heavy dark beard sprinkled with gray now covered his face. But the sound of his voice had remained the same, as had the smile that spread across his face. Jeff had also changed. At twelve, he was much taller and more mature. And the bright blue eyes he inherited from his mother distinguished him from other passengers.

"You look like a Latin scholar," Isaac said to Jeff, who was still wearing his school uniform. "Unfortunately, we must spend the night at a boarding house. It's too late in the evening to travel to Rosemont. We can't stay with Joseph because he is away from Natchez, and he won't return until morning."

"You could stay at my uncle's home," Charles said. "It's just off the main street, and he won't mind if I bring two guests with me."

"I appreciate your offer, but I don't want to inconvenience anyone."

"No problem at all. He lives alone since his wife died last summer. His children live in Natchez, but they are married and have their own households. The home is now empty of family members, and he has invited me to board with him."

Isaac and Jeff barely had time to unpack before they heard the dinner bell ring downstairs. The dining table was set with imported china and the food on display was more sumptuous than Jeff had seen at school during the last two years. The conversation that evening centered on a region called Texas. Settlers from the Southern States had started trickling into the Mexican territory.

"I believe there'll soon be a flood of Americans going there," Isaac said.

"Not likely," Charles said. "It will always be just a trickle. The authorities down there require any immigrant to swear an oath that he is a Catholic. Americans don't want the land enough to give up their Protestant faith."

"But what makes you think we won't take it by force someday?" Charles' uncle asked.

"Because there's still too much land available in Mississippi and Alabama," Charles said.

Listening to the conversation, Jeff was puzzled. He didn't understand why someone would turn down land if all you had to do was become a Catholic.

The next morning Isaac and Jeff set out for home. When they reached the crossroads near Rosemont, Isaac said, "Jeff, you go ahead to the house. I'm going to Woodville and take care of some pressing matters." After Isaac disappeared from view, Jeff dug his heels into the ribs of his horse and set out for home. Soon he spotted the plantation in the distance. He had been away from his family for a long time. For a brief moment he lost control of his emotions and tears flowed down his face. The calloused exterior he had developed simply could not hold his feelings. He pressed his heels into the side of the horse, and the animal responded by trotting at a fast pace down the tree-lined avenue.

Much to Jeff's surprise, no one came out to meet him. He stopped in front of the house and tied the reins of the horse to a small pine sapling. When he walked around to the back entrance, he saw his mother sitting near the door, shelling butter beans. At first she did not hear his approach because a fever last spring had left her partially deaf. He stood and gazed at her for a moment. She must have felt his presence for she turned her head in his direction.

"Jeff," she screamed out when she saw him.

Jane's feet raced the short distance between them. She wrapped her arms around his frame and pulled him to her breasts.

"We were expecting you yesterday."

"The steamboat was late arriving in Natchez, so we spent the night there."

"Where's Isaac?"

"He left me at the crossroads. Said he had to get to Woodville to take care of some business."

"Yes, and I know her name."

"Where is everyone?"

"Your sisters are at the Dempsey farm. But they will be home for supper."

"Where's Pa?"

"He's out in the fields. You best go see him."

Jeff took an old Indian trail that meandered through the woods until it ended where the cotton was planted. When he reached the edge of the forest he saw his father, sitting on his horse, directing the slaves in their task. Jeff stood there frozen in his tracks for a moment. He did not know how to approach him. Should he shake his hand or embrace him? His father was a good man, but not one who often showed any outward affection.

Samuel saw Jeff walk into the field from the trees that bordered it. He dismounted and met him at a pine stump near the corner of the cotton patch.

"Papa," Jeff said, and stuck out his hand for his father to shake. But Samuel was too overcome with emotion for that to satisfy his need. Ignoring the outstretched hand, he embraced his son. Samuel could hardly muster the strength to keep tears from busting forth. A moment later, he returned to his reserved self.

* * *

When fall came, Jeff was sent off to school again. But this time it was in the next county. Jefferson Academy, like Jeff, was named after the American President. During his time there, he and the other boys suffered beatings when they failed to achieve what the school master expected. One day Jeff was given an assignment that he felt was too difficult, and because he dreaded a beating, he went to see his father in the fields and complained.

"Jeff, you must have decided to be a common laborer instead of an educated man. Tomorrow you will stay home and pick cotton."

The next morning Samuel took Jeff to the fields and handed him a crocus bag with a shoulder strap.

"Get to work in the field, and I will see you come supper time."

It was hard work, and Jeff was the only free person picking cotton. He was amazed how the Negroes could laugh, sing, carry on animated conversations, and still pick cotton faster than he could. At the end of the day his pile of cotton almost matched the others, but it was only because they had helped him pick his rows. Exhausted, Jeff left the field as the sun began to set. That evening home was a welcomed sight. When he entered the kitchen, his mother was busy setting the table. He noticed that his father was not around.

"Where's Papa?" he asked.

"He's in Woodville at the Agriculture Club," his mother replied.

Jeff knew the club meeting was something that his father enjoyed attending. Its membership was composed of planters who wanted to exchange the latest information about cotton growing. His father was always trying new methods to increase the amount he could produce. After supper, Jeff tried to stay awake until his father came home. But when he began to nod, his mother sent him to bed.

Samuel was late getting home that evening, and by the time he arrived, Jeff was already fast asleep. The next morning Jeff was up early. Before his father could inquire if he had made a decision about what path he planned to take in life, Jeff was on his way to school where the assignments did not seem so difficult anymore.

The next year Jeff transferred to a school that was opening its doors for the first time that fall. Wilkinson County Academy was only six miles from Rosemont. The head-master was from Boston and held a long list of scholarly accomplishments. For the first time, Jeff was to receive an education that did not center on the use of a whip to encourage learning.

Despite his new attraction for books, Jeff found time to continue his favorite past time of hunting and fishing. He always had several hunting dogs to which he showed great affection. But his favorite animal was the horse. His father had purchased him a stallion that was chestnut in color, and Jeff named him Jackson after the general. Like his father, Jeff was born to the saddle and soon developed a reputation in the community for good horsemanship. He thought nothing of riding the twenty miles to visit his sister, Anna, at her plantation, Locust Grove.

During the next three years while attending the academy, Jeff became well-versed in Greek and Latin. During the same time he was learning Spanish with his friend John Quitman.

At this period of his life, Jeff greatly admired his brother, Joseph, and decided he would follow him in the law. To prepare him for that, his father promised to send him once again to Kentucky. This time he would be attending Transylvania University in Lexington. The week before Jeff left, his father departed for Philadelphia with his servant, James Pemberton. Samuel hoped to ease his pressing debts by contacting his relatives there about interest he might have in his grandfather's estate. Jeff had no way of knowing that he would never see his father again.

* * *

Lexington was a prosperous town that rivaled Natchez. This bustling center of trade was filled with stately mansions, and was often called the Athens of the South. The university was located in the heart of town, and was the pride of the region. Many of its graduates would later hold high political office. Friendships forged there by Jeff would stand the test of time. Even the War Between the States would not destroy them.

There were no dormitories on campus, so the students boarded with families in town who accepted renters. Jeff had a room on the corner of High and Limestone Streets at the home of Mr. Ficklin. He was an old friend of Jeff's father. Mrs. Ficklin treated him like a member of the family and made his stay during his school years in Lexington a pleasant one.

Illness stalked his family while Jeff was away. His sister, Mary Ellen, died of an unspecified cause. This was followed by news that Isaac's wife, Susannah, had become terminally ill. Shortly after learning this bad news, Jeff received word that his father, Samuel, had passed away from the fever in July at the age of sixty-one. Although the character of his father had been such as to deter him from often embracing his children, he had their respect. Later in life, Jeff would seem withdrawn and unattached when faced with a crisis, a characteristic he had inherited from his father.

By the time of his death, Samuel had lost everything. His years of hard work had disappeared before his eyes. This downfall resulted from his signature as a guarantor on a note for his son-in-law. When his daughter's husband failed to pay, Samuel's farm and home were in danger of being seized to satisfy the debt. Only Joseph's intervention saved the day. He assumed the debt in return for the title to his father's home and land. But he allowed his father and mother to continue to live at Rosemont and to farm the place.

* * *

Jeff had looked forward to his senior year at the university in Lexington. But his plans to graduate and then study law at the University of Virginia were dashed when his brother, Joseph, arrived for a visit.

"Jeff, there's not any assets in Father's estate."

"How will my tuition be paid for next year?"

"There's no money for that. I can get you an appointment to West Point."

"Why would I go there? I want to graduate from Transylvania and then pursue the study of law at the University of Virginia."

"West Point does not require tuition, and you will receive a monthly allowance from the government, once you are sworn in as a cadet."

"I thought we were going to practice law together."

"It's not as lucrative as it used to be. Mississippi is flooded with lawyers. I'm quitting the practice of law and intend to focus my energies on becoming a successful planter. Right now, I'm deep in debt, but I need only three successful cotton season to pay off my creditors. After that, I shall become a wealthy planter like our father always wanted to be. You, on the other hand, must find a respectable profession. An officer in the United States Army is an honorable endeavor for one without wealth."

"If there's no other way."

Jeff did not want to take this path, but since he was without funds to complete his courses at Transylvania, he had no choice.

The following month he received a commission signed by the Secretary of War, John C. Calhoun. Unfortunately, it was mistakenly sent to Natchez and only arrived in Lexington in July. Even after its arrival, Jeff delayed his trip to the academy because he hated to leave his friends at Transylvania.

WEST POINT ACADEMY AND SERVICE IN THE UNITED STATES ARMY

On September 15th, Jeff finally reached his destination in New York State. The nation's military academy had a student body of 259 students, and the campus covered only a small portion of the vast acres owned by the United States Government. As Jeff approached the administration building, he saw a gentleman in uniform.

"Where is the admissions office?"

"Who are you?"

"Jefferson Davis from Mississippi. I've a commission as a freshman cadet."

The officer gave him a questioning look and shook his head before pointing to the door of an imposing structure nearby. Upon entering the building, he saw an officer locking the door of the admissions office. When the man turned around, Jeff handed him the commission signed by the Secretary of War.

"You are too late to register for this year. The deadline was the first day of September."

"I was delayed. My commission was sent to Natchez. But I was in Lexington at Transylvania University."

"Natchez," Captain Hitchcock said, as he perused the commission. "Do you know Joseph Davis?"

"He's my brother."

"I stopped in Natchez once when I was on a military assignment. He was kind enough to allow me to stay at his home while I was in the area. Your brother is a gentleman of the highest order. Come with me to the mess hall. It's time for the mid-day meal. Afterwards, we shall go see the superintendent. Perhaps we can convince him to make an exception in your case."

The office of the superintendent was on the second floor of the administration building. In the office was a senior cadet who helped Colonel Thayer with the paper work that all bureaucracies have known since the rise of civilization.

"Is the Colonel in?" Captain Hitchcock asked.

"He's just returned from an inspection tour."

"Cadet Davis and I need to speak to him."

The colonel, hearing voices outside his door, stepped into the outer office.

"What is it, Captain?" he asked.

"This is Cadet Jefferson Davis. He's just arrived."

"A little late for enrollment this year."

"Could I have a private audience with you on this matter?"

"Mr. Davis, wait out here," Hitchcock said.

In the privacy of his quarters Colonel Thayer said, "Captain, you know the rule."

"The boy's commission was misdirected," Captain Hitchcock responded. "He's a good candidate for our academy. I met his brother once in Natchez, an important man in that state. He was a member of the Mississippi Convention that petitioned the congress for statehood. His family has a long history of service to this country. His father, Samuel, fought in the American Revolution, and two of Jeff's brothers fought in the War of 1812 at New Orleans under Major Hinds."

"There is already a young man taking a special examination tomorrow," Thayer said. "He was in Europe, and was delayed in his return to the States through no fault of his own. There would be no harm since the faculty is already scheduled for one special examination. We will simply have them examine this young man afterwards. If Davis passes, he's in. Otherwise, the young man can take his leave and return to Mississippi."

The test was easy for Jeff. His time at Lexington had given him a basic knowledge of algebra, geometry, French, and Greek. Many of the other cadets did not have the advantages that Jeff's father had provided for him in the family household, as well as the formal education he had received since the age of seven.

"You passed that with ease," Hitchcock said the next morning when Jeff came by his office.

Jeff noticed that in the corner of the room was his military issue.

"Place your hand upon the Bible on my desk so that I may administer the cadet oath, which will subject you to active duty immediately if the need should arise, and it commits you to service in the Army after graduation."

"I, Jefferson Davis, of the State of Mississippi, age seventeen years, having been selected for an appointment as Cadet in the Military Academy of these United States, do hereby engage, with the consent of my Brother Joseph Davis,

my guardian, and having received my appointment from the Secretary of War, that I will serve in the Army of these United States for Five Years unless sooner discharged by competent authority. And, I Jefferson Davis, do solemnly swear that I will bear true allegiance to these United States of America, and that I will serve them honestly and faithfully against all their enemies whatsoever, and observe and obey the orders of the President and the officers appointed over me, according to the Rules and Articles of War."

"You have been assigned to room with Walter Guion," Hitchcock said. "He's from your home state. Perhaps you can keep him from the type of trouble he has been getting into lately. If you can't, it won't bode well for him. The number of demerits he has received indicates that he's on a path that will lead to his dismissal."

Jeff got along well with his roommate. Walter enjoyed having a good time, and before long Jeff was joining Walter and other cadets at Benny Haven's tavern, an establishment off campus. This was a violation of school regulations. The demerits against Jeff's name began to mount, and the costs of joining his friends left him short of money. Soon he found himself composing a letter to Joseph requesting him to send funds. He kept this secret since cadets were prohibited from obtaining monies from outside sources. Cadets were expected to live within the allowance given by the government. But all the cadets, except those from the most impoverished families, maintained their life styles by outside sources.

The first year was particularly difficult because Jeff did not want to be at the academy. It galled Jeff that he had to start as a freshman, even though he had already finished three years at Transylvania. Now all thoughts of attending the University of Virginia where he could study law were dashed when correspondences from Joseph convinced him that his only option was to pursue a military career. He yielded to that persuasion, but emotionally he rebelled. His conduct at West Point clearly reflected that he was on a path that he did not want to take. The only outlet for his relief was drinking and playing cards at Benny Havens' tavern.

Jeff's circle of friends came from members of his class, except for Albert Sidney Johnson. Although Sidney was the oldest cadet at the school, he befriended Jeff when he discovered that Jeff had attended the university in Lexington where Sidney had graduated.

During his first year, Jeff developed new interests. When he was unable to slip off campus, he read poetry, studied architecture, and drew sketches. His drawings were of such high caliber that soon his fellow cadets were asking him to compose pictures of them to send to their family. Often in class when a professor was vigorously lecturing, Jeff was either composing a poem or drawing. If a professor took notice, he just thought Jeff was busy taking notes.

In Jeff's second year, things began to improve when Benny Haven's daughter came to work there. A girl of fifteen, she waited on tables at her father's establishment. For young men in their prime isolated from females, she was an immediate attraction. She enjoyed the attention of the cadets, but she was particularly taken with the blue-eyed six-foot-framed cadet from Mississippi, Jefferson Davis and a cadet from Virginia, Joseph Johnson, who would later become a famous confederate general. Benny always kept a watchful eye on his daughter, and any cadet who crossed the line found himself banished from the establishment for a time. Eventually, Jeff and Joseph realized that she had chosen them as her favorites, and each tried to outdo the other in attracting her attention.

One evening when Jeff and Joseph had too much drink, words were exchanged, and for the first time Jeff found himself in a physical confrontation. After each had delivered several blows, the two found themselves fighting and kicking on the hardwood floor like two common ruffians. They were finally separated, and Benny banished them for a month. When their exile was over, they returned to the tavern and discovered their attraction had been sent to live with an aunt in New Jersey. Although neither man would ever see her again, Jeff would always remember her as his first love, and he would never reconcile with Joseph Johnson.

Jeff added another friend during his second year at the academy when he reached out to a freshman named Robert E Lee. The Virginian was different from the other cadets. He never went to Haven's Tavern and seemed focused on graduating at the top of his class. Everyone knew his father, Light Horse Harry Lee, had a bad reputation for strong drink and other unacceptable practices. They assumed Lee was very rigid in his conduct in order to draw a sharp distinction between his father and him. There were many others in Jeff's wide circle of friends, including Leonidas Polk who had a public conversion in front of the cadets during service at the chapel one Sunday morning. These friendships that Jeff formed were for life, and no one could have imagined as the world changed how these connections would affect a coming conflict in America.

By his third year Jeff had accepted the fact that a military career was the path his life would take, but he still rebelled against those in authority. During the Christmas season that year, the students wanted to celebrate, but it was forbidden by the officers. A group of cadets chose to ignore authority. They selected Jeff to slip down to Havens' after dark and secure whiskey and eggs for the purpose of making traditional Christmas egg-nog drinks. After the monies were collected from fellow cadets, he left the campus and walked through a snow storm to accomplish his mission. The cold wind had chilled him to the bone by the time he reached his destination, despite the fact that he had on a heavy military overcoat and a double pair of woolen socks. He tarried at the tavern for a couple of hours until the snow stopped falling, and the heat from the blazing fireplace had dried articles of clothing he had removed. He had a few drinks with other patrons, and enjoyed the company of a barmaid recently employed at Havens before facing the brutal weather outside again.

* * *

"What took you so long?" Guion asked.
"I waited for the weather to clear."

Guidon could smell whiskey on Jeff, but he chose not to chastise him for the delay.

"Let's get this down to James Sevier's room."

When they arrived, cadets were anxiously waiting outside in the hallway. Someone joked that everyone thought Jeff had fled the academy with their money. While the brew was concocted, a large group of about seventy cadets gathered outside. As the group became even larger, they decided to go to the assembly room on the first floor. Soon everyone was indulging, and after a few drinks a cadet led the others in singing popular tunes of the day.

At one a. m. Jeff said to Guion, "I feel sick." Then he rushed down the hallway and out into the snow, where he vomited. Becoming deathly ill from the alcohol consumed, Jeff entered the dormitory through a different entrance and went directly to his room. Lying on his bed made his condition seemed even worst. The room was spinning. He stood up and went to the bathroom down the hall, where he vomited until he was having dry heaves.

A cadet from his class entered the bathroom.

"Jeff, you had better get to your room. Captain Hitchcock is outside patrolling the grounds, and he may come into this building."

"I've got to warn Guion and the others," Jeff said.

He stumbled to the assembly room.

"Get to your rooms, Hitchcock is about."

Then he saw the captain standing there.

"Davis, you're drunk. Go directly to your room and remain there."

Jeff staggered to his room where he passed out when his head hit the pillow.

* * *

Standing on the parade ground, Jeff was pleased that he was graduating. In his senior year, he had been on his best behavior. He had been lucky not to have been dismissed from the academy. His roommate, Guion, and eighteen others had been found guilty of what would be remembered as The Egg-Nog Riot that broke out after Jeff had been ordered to his room. The riot had turned so violent that the cadets involved had driven the officers out of their barracks and pursued them to the officers' quarters. In the physical fight that followed, chairs had been broken and weapons presented. Jeff had only been saved from involvement in the violence by the fact that he was under arrest in his room and asleep when the riot took place. His punishment for furnishing the liquor and being drunk was a reprimanded and placement under six week's arrest.

The four years at the academy had changed Jeff, as it would any man. He was ready to be commissioned as a brevet lieutenant and receive his assignment for duty. In a graduating class of thirty-three, his academic ranking was twenty-three. This meant he would be relegated to infantry, while the top ranked would be assigned to civil engineering. Even at this late stage, his natural interest did not lie in the military but in the law, reading, poetry, drawing, and architecture. Until he was actually involved in a conflict, he would find no great pleasure in soldiering.

The academy gave each graduating cadet a sixty-day leave before they received orders assigning them to their post. During his leave, Jeff decided to accept an invitation from a fellow graduate, Thomas Drayton. This friend's uncle had a rice plantation near the port of Georgetown in South Carolina. Thomas and Jeff took a coach to Providence, Rhode Island where they stayed a few days with Thomas' sister, who was spending the summer with relatives to escape the heat of the South Carolina coast. Then the two boarded a ship for Charleston. It was a pleasant journey, and the passengers were lucky the sudden storms that frequently visited the Atlantic failed to appear during their trip. The ship landed at the port city, and Thomas booked a room in a hotel, after hiring a rider to take a message to his uncle announcing they had arrived.

"I'm sure he will send his sloop to get us," Thomas said.

During the three days that the two waited for the sloop, they visited the grounds being prepared for a military college, The Citadel. The impetus for the school was an attempted slave revolt by a free Negro named Denmark Vesey. The plot had been uncovered in time by a loyal slave who told his master. The well-organized plot had even included members of the governor's household. In the future, the Citadel would house an armed force of white men that could be called out on a moment's notice to provide immediate protection until the militia could be aroused.

Jeff was impressed with the architecture in Charleston. Not only were the homes well designed, but the two principal houses of worship, Saint Michaels and Saint Phillips, so inspired Jeff that he sketched them.

One morning the two men received a message that the boat had arrived. They went down to the dock and boarded her. The weather was beautiful and a breeze filled her sail. In the afternoon the ship reached the mouth of Winyah Bay. Unfortunately, it was low tide, and the entrance to the bay was so shallow that they had to wait for the water to rise.

When the boat entered the bay, Jeff observed the vast rice fields. Unlike Mississippi, the wealth on the South Carolina coast was accumulated by cultivating rice instead of planting cotton. He would later learn that whereas a large cotton plantation might have three hundred slaves, rice required more labor. It was not unusual to have two thousand slaves in the rice fields of a plantation during the harvest.

Soon Georgetown came into view. A city of three thousand, it stretched along the bank near the mouth of the Sampit River. The stores and warehouses that lined the wharf also had entrances to a public highway called Front Street.

Since the hour was late, Thomas suggested they wait until morning before commencing their journey up the Waccamaw River to his uncle's plantation. After inquiring, they decided to stay at the Cleland Tavern. The establishment had rooms for rent upstairs. It was only a block from the water-front and near a courthouse which had been constructed by Robert Mills, a famous architect.

"You will like my uncle and his family," Thomas said as the small boat skimmed across the surface of the water the next day. On a distant bluff, Jeff saw a home that faced the river. When the boat entered a tributary and docked, a houseboy greeted them. While he held the reins of the horses, they mounted them. Then Thomas and Jeff followed him, as he ran along a trail that led to the plantation home of his master. As they approached, Jeff was impressed by the sight of a beautiful flower garden that spread endlessly in front of the home. On the veranda stood an old man surrounded by three women.

"Welcome," the man said as they dismounted. "One of my slaves brought us word that you were coming around the bend of the river."

"Uncle John, I want you to meet my good friend, Jefferson Davis."

As Jeff felt the firm grip of John Pawley's hand, the three ladies came down the steps of the veranda and walked toward them.

"My daughters, Isabel, Mary, and Constance," the old man said.

The older two were rather plain, but the young one, Constance, a girl of sixteen, took Jeff's breathe away. After their trunks were unpacked in a comfortable room upstairs, they joined John for mint juleps at a table under an ancient live oak tree. The branches provided shade, and the breeze that blew up from the river kept the insects at bay. Later that evening, the men joined the ladies for dinner in a large dining room. Everything on the table was silver, china, or porcelain. Jeff could see that the wealth of a rice planter far exceeded anything that a cotton planter could ever dream of accumulating.

The following days were spent hunting wild pigs which had become so prolific, they were a threat to the cultivated crops. Jeff was also able to enjoy fishing in the river. In the evenings the family gathered in the library for conversation. Jeff enjoyed the nightly discussions, for the entire family seemed well-versed on matters that carried far beyond their world. During these discussions, he was especially attracted to Constance who seemed to listen to every word that dropped from his lips.

During his stay, Jeff learned a great deal about his host. John was a widower. The two oldest girls were from his first wife who died of the fever.

Afterwards, he had married a young woman who had recently arrived in Charleston from France. Although she was of the Catholic faith, he had persuaded her to marry him, but her consent did not come easy. He had to struggle during a long courtship to overcome her resistance to his age and to his Protestant faith. A year after they were married, she died while giving birth to Constance. He had chosen not to marry again. Instead, he devoted himself to raising his daughters. The oldest one was now engaged to a neighboring planter. With the social season beginning in Charleston soon, he expected that his second daughter would have a proposal before Christmas.

Walking the gardens alone one day, Jeff heard his name spoken. He turned to see Constance step out from behind a tree.

"I didn't mean to startle you," she said.

Jeff could see that Constance was nervous. It was not considered proper for an unmarried girl to be alone with a man who was not family. She had somehow escaped the watchful eyes of the household mammy and apparently had waited for him to take his customary walk on the grounds. The beautiful dress she wore exposed the top portions of her breasts, which stirred him.

"Your family would not think it proper for us to be alone," he said as he walked toward her.

"My father and Thomas are out riding and my sisters are on the boat sailing downriver to a neighbor's plantation."

"Where's your Mammy?"

"Visiting the slave quarters. One of her sisters is sick."

By this time she stood very close to him, and he could smell the scent of yellow jessamine emitting from her body. He felt his heart begin to beat fast as his hand reached out and took hers.

"Should we stroll about the garden?" he asked.

She did not respond, but together they walked down to a grove of trees that stood some distance from the house. When they were away from prying eyes, she stopped and turned her face up to his.

"Do you want to kiss me?" she asked.

The tone of her voice showed that she did not expect a reply but only some action on his part. Jeff had not kissed a woman since Julie at Haven's Tavern. Constance's lips were so inviting that he could not restrain himself. He leaned forward and pressed his lips to hers. Her arms went around his neck, and he could feel the contours of her body crush against him.

"I love you, Jeff," she said.

Jeff did not respond, but his hands reached up and covered her young breasts. She let out a groan, and her body began to shiver. Then she tore away from him, with the look of one whom had not expected her actions to have invoked such a response.

"We must go back to the house," she said as she stepped away from his embrace. "Will you come again to visit us?" she asked just before they parted ways near the home.

"Yes," he said, because he knew that answer would please her.

"Will you write when you reach your military posting, so that I can have an address to correspond with you?"

This was the only time they were alone before the end of his visit, but Constance managed to press a note in his hand one afternoon that contained a sufficient address to contact her.

The two-week stay had been a wonderful experience, but the Pawley family and Thomas were traveling to Charleston to spend the rest of the summer. Jeff joined them on the sloop to the Holy City where he was able to book passage to Wilmington. From there, he took a coach to Lexington. Although his friends at Transylvania University had graduated, his purpose in returning was to spend time with the Ficklins. They had treated him like family the three years he had lived in their home. Besides, he hoped to see their daughter, Betsey, with whom he had a relationship while he lived in their home.

Jeff delayed going to Rosemont until it was fever season in Mississippi. Then using that danger as an excuse, he wrote to General Winfield Scott and requested an extension of his furlough. He received an order, signed by the general's aide, Samuel Cooper, granting his request. Attached to that order was a directive requiring him to report during December to Jefferson Barracks, a post near St. Louis. In the early fall he left Lexington for Mississippi.

Seven years had passed since Jeff last visited Rosemont. Now only his mother and his sister, Lucinda Stamps, with her family, lived there. His mother was now entering her twilight years, and she had been deprived of her son's presence for most of her life.

Rosemount had not prospered under Joseph's care. He had neglected it while he established his plantation, *Hurricane*, on the Mississippi at a place later called Davis Bend by the local inhabitants. Joseph took a few days off from supervising the clearing of the forest and came to Rosemont to see his brother. He brought his new wife, Eliza, and his slave James Pemberton. The next day Joseph's three daughters arrived, and Jeff was introduced to them for the first time.

Jeff returned with Joseph to *Hurricane* which was still not completed, though Joseph and his family had already moved into it. There he spent a few days before returning to Rosemont. He observed in his older brother, Joseph, all the things he admired. He was an intellectual giant in his state and held the respect of those who came into contact with him. Now he was on the verge of realizing his dream of becoming a successful planter and taking his place in the top hierarchy of the state. During the days spent with Joseph, Jeff, for the first time, developed an interest in politics. His brother was well-versed on these matters, not only on local issues but also on national concerns.

"How could Joseph exercise such good judgment in other matters and then make such a poor choice in choosing a wife?" Jeff asked his mother one day after returning to Rosemont. "Eliza is only sixteen and Joseph is forty-three. He's never been married before and now has gathered under one roof at *Hurricane* his daughters by three different women and a bride."

"It is beyond me," she replied. "I suspect it has to do with his age. Now that he has accumulated wealth, perhaps he realizes that family is more important. But I suspect there will be tremendous stress in that household with the dynamic of four women suddenly thrown together."

The last day of his stay at Rosemont, Joseph returned with his wife and three daughters. They sat down for a fine dinner that Jane's cooks had prepared. Despite his concerns, Jeff liked the daughters. Afterwards, as the two men sat out on the porch. Joseph handed Jeff a document.

"What's this?"

"A deed conveying James to you. He's trustworthy. I know the army allows each officer a servant. I want you to have him as a gift from me. You have made our family proud."

"Have you spoken to James about this?"

"He is reconciled to leaving."

James lay awake that night and gazed at the stars from beneath a tree where he had laid a thick blanket for his bed. He would need to be up at the rise of dawn and saddle the two horses. In Natchez, Mr. Jeff and he would board a steamer for St. Louis.

During his early years, James had spent his days as a boy in the kitchen where his mother had been the cook for Jane Davis' family. Although, on occasion, Jeff and he had hunted and fished together, he didn't know him well because his new master had spent most of his life away from home.

Despite some misgivings about leaving the area, things had already begun to change in James' world. His master, Samuel, had died, and he had ended up with Joseph, who had taken on a family and was now living on the new plantation. His roots at Rosemont had been slowly stripped away, since his Mother's death. He had begun to feel like a stranger both at Rosemont and at Joseph's place. He had no wife to hold on to. There were children hereabout that might be his, but he had never laid a claim to any. So he was at a point in his life that made it easy for him to accept the change being placed upon him. Even if he had felt different, it would not have mattered. He was a slave and not in control of his own life. His destiny was always in the hands of a master.

* * *

Jeff and James spent only a short time at the post near St. Louis. There, Jeff was reunited with several friends who had reported months earlier.

"Jeff, what kept you?" Albert Sidney Johnson asked. "All the pretty girls have been taken."

"I delayed so you would get first pick," Jeff said.

"I'm glad you have finally arrived," Sidney said. "All that Thomas Drayton thinks of are women. It will be good to have someone to engage in intellectual discussions for a change. Most of the officers only want to drink and play cards."

"Well, I'm not opposed to that," Jeff said as a smile spread across his face.

During Jeff's stay there, he received infantry training before being ordered to Fort Crawford where he was attached to the First Infantry Regiment. The fort lay near the Mississippi in the Michigan Territory beyond Illinois. He was there only a few weeks before the commanding officer ordered him to Fort Winnebago to assist Major Twiggs in finishing its construction. Because lumber was needed, the major placed Jeff in command of a company to cut timber on the upper Wisconsin. Once the timber was cut, the logs would be floated down the river to the fort.

In late July 1831, Jeff and his infantry company arrived on the Yellow River. The men were undisciplined, and the largest man in the group got drunk the first night of their encampment. In a loud voice he threatened to whip Jeff and anyone else who tried to give him orders. Jeff knew the men were watching him, and if he didn't take forceful action, he would have a mutiny on his hands. He eyed a stack of logs near the fire. He jumped atop the logs and struck the man with the full force of his right fist. The soldier fell to the ground unconscious. With this one act, he gained the infantrymen's respect and would have no further trouble getting them to obey orders.

Jeff had brought some trade goods with him. Soon friendly Indians visited their site and in exchange for American goods they brought fresh meat for the men each day. This saved the company from the need to organize parties to go in search of food. Thus, they were able to devote their complete attention to cutting trees.

In late fall the weather turned intensely cold, and Jeff caught pneumonia. He was unable to leave the small wooden hut the men had constructed as his quarters. James stayed by his side and nursed him back from the edge of death. During this time he lost weight, became dehydrated, and so weakened he could not leave his cot. On the third day he developed a severe pain in his left eye, and for a while he went totally blind in that eye.

Jeff had the sergeant come by twice a day to his quarters and give him reports on the progress of their mission. The Indian leaders also visited him and were amazed that despite his illness, Jeff stayed focused on his duties. They began to call him Little Chief because he had become just skin and bone. A tribal leader sent his young daughter to do the cooking and make herbal soup. At night this fifteen-year-old maiden slept under the covers beside him to keep his body warm. Soon his strength returned, and he was finally able to go outside to supervise the work. But he never completely recovered. From this experience, he was always plagued with health problems.

One day Jeff took three men with him up river to do some hunting. After they had found a good place and disembarked some Indians came around the bend.

"Let's trade with them," Jeff said.

Jeff and his men untied their craft and paddled in the Indian's direction. When they got close, they realized that this was not a tribe they had dealt with before at the camp. In just a few moments they were being chased down the river, and the hostile Indians were gaining on them.

"We are going to be overtaken," Jeff said. "Their canoes are faster than our craft."

Then a thought occurred to him on how they might increase their speed.

"Hand me those two extra oars and the large blanket."

He fashioned a temporary sail from a blanket by attaching it to the extra oars, which he had wedged into the spaces between the boards of the craft. The wind was blowing hard and soon the craft picked up enough speed to enable them to escape.

The mission completed, Jeff and his men were ordered back to Fort Crawford. When Jeff arrived, there were new orders awaiting him. His company was to immediately depart for Dubuque's Mines in Iowa territory. Miners had trespassed on Indian lands in search of lead. The recent discovery of deep deposits of this rare item had led to a surge of numerous settlers into the area seeking their fortune. A treaty was pending in the United States Senate that would cede this property to the government. Until the treaty was ratified, it was Jeff's job to move the miners back across the river and prevent others from establishing camps.

There had already been incidents with the Indians and Washington was afraid of a full scale war if the mining was not stopped. When he arrived, news reached him that the miners already established in the tribal areas had threatened to resist removal. Later he learned of a plot to kill him. Jeff, with only a company under his command, knew he could not force the miners to leave if they were inclined to resist. He sent word that he was coming to their main camp for a meeting. In the meantime, he personally visited the homes of several individuals. At the meeting later that week, he calmly explained that the treaty with the tribes would soon be approved.

"I will put into the hands of the government each individual claim so that late comers cannot take advantage from your departure."

When Jeff first began to speak, he could feel their anger and was interrupted by hostile comments. In the end, he persuaded them to leave the area with a promise that he would take their mining claims to the authorities. Three months later the treaty was approved, and the miners were allowed to return.

After he was back at Fort Crawford, Jeff put in for a furlough. While the slow bureaucracy took its time with his paper work, several incidents with the Indians occurred in the territories. One of them involved a raid on a farm house where a young female child was taken. Jeff was ordered to retrieve her. After accomplishing the mission, Jeff and Lieutenant Robert Anderson were sent to Fort Dixson, Illinois with supplies for the militia which had been organized to defend settlers from Indian attacks. Upon their arrival, they administered the oath to the officers elected by the militia companies. One of the officers was Abraham Lincoln who had been elected captain by his men. While Jeff administered the oath, Robert Anderson held the bible on which Lincoln placed his hand. He was a tall, gawky, homely man, dressed in a cotton shirt and blue jeans. Although the man made no impression on him, Lincoln would always say that the first oath he ever took was one administered by Jefferson Davis.

When Jeff returned to Fort Crawford, he spent time with several officers with whom he had become friends. Their conversations focused on the Nullification Act of South Carolina which had threatened to ignore the Federal Tariff Act. President Jackson had Congress pass the Force Act. And now he was threatening to send the Army into South Carolina to enforce the law. The state had responded by calling out the militia. No one could be sure how this matter would end. After giving it considerable thought, Jeff wrote a letter to his brother.

"Joseph, I would resign my commission before I shed the blood of citizens of another state. The rest of the officers are divided on where their loyalty would lie if the president tries to use military force against a state. A majority believes their oath is to these United States and not to the federal government in Washington."

Finally the furlough was granted. Jeff and James left Fort Crawford the next day. They arrived in Woodville the first part of April. He expected to spend considerable time with his brother, Joseph, and the other members of his family.

* * *

Joseph's home, *Hurricane*, was located on his plantation along the Mississippi. The name had attached to the structure after his brother, Samuel Jr., suffered a broken leg and the death of his two children during a hurricane that struck the house while it was under construction. Samuel left the plantation and never returned, believing God had cursed the place.

Hurricane having been completed, Joseph was in the process of closing his law practice so he could devote himself to the plantation. Jeff spent time there with Joseph and his family. He had long discussions with his brother about his future. He felt that perhaps the Army was not the place where he could find his full potential. Promotion was slow in an Army that was very small. The success of his brother made him restless to create his own wealth. Joseph listened carefully but never committed to help him in another career.

When Jeff heard that an Indian war had erupted near Fort Crawford, he cut short his furlough and departed Mississippi. He arrived at his post in August. By that time the Indians had been defeated. However, the instigator, Chief Black Hawk, had escaped with several of his warriors.

Word reached the fort that the chief and his party had been spotted. Jeff and Robert Anderson set forth with a company of men to capture him. They discovered the Indians' camp a few miles north of Fort Crawford near the Mississippi. When the detachment approached, the Indians raised a white flag and were taken into custody without any resistance.

Jeff delivered the captives to his commander, who immediately had them shackled and put in the stockade. The next week when a steamboat stopped, Jeff was ordered to take the captives aboard the ship for transport to Fort Armstrong at Rock Island. Once the ship was underway, Jeff had the shackles removed from the chief. He treated him with dignity, and the chief reciprocated by giving him a pipe his son had made. Since Jeff had learned the dialect of his tribe, the two men were able to converse about the war. When they arrived at Rock Island, Jeff discovered an epidemic of cholera had broken out. The commander, General Winfield Scott, ordered the captives taken further south to Jefferson Barracks. During the trip two warriors became ill with cholera which they had contracted during their short stay at Fort Armstrong. They begged to be put ashore so they could die in the land of their ancestors. Jeff took pity on them and had them transferred by canoe to a small island. For a few minutes after the steamboat got underway again, the passengers could hear the dying chants of the men. After completing his duty, Jeff returned to Fort Crawford in September.

* * *

After the nullification crisis, Fort Crawford received a new commanding officer. Zachary Taylor was disappointed at the unfinished state of the fort upon his arrival in the autumn of 1831. Several officers and their families were still living in tents. He issued orders to improve the condition of existing structures and build new ones. This construction included the enlargement of his own quarters to accommodate his family of three daughters and a son, through his youngest daughter, Sarah, was not with them. She was still attending school in Cincinnati.

Jeff got along well with his new commanding officer. He admired his professionalism and foresight in issuing the necessary directives to carry out the mission of the First Infantry Regiment. Colonel Taylor in return admired the way Jeff handled himself with the enlisted men, and the common sense he used when he was assigned a mission. On several occasions, he invited Jeff to join his family at their evening meal. An invitation he rarely extended to the other officers.

It was the Christmas season of 1832, and the big social event for the holidays was a Christmas party given by Colonel Taylor. All officers and the prominent members of the community were invited. A newly constructed building that still lay empty was used for this occasion. Jeff and the other men looked forward to something that would help break the monotony of life at a frontier post during the winter months.

The night of the party, Jeff and Sidney Johnson stood in a corner of the room and drank locally brewed whiskey. They watched couples dance and listened to the music being played by a traveling group of musicians.

"I think you ought to ask Mary Tyler to dance one more time. You know she has taken a fancy to you."

This bit of information was not news to Jeff. The seventeen-year-old, whose father was a merchant, never missed an opportunity to visit the fort. She always managed to find Jeff and speak with him on those occasions. Earlier that evening, her father had invited him to join the family for dinner at mid-day on Christmas and to stay the week. Anything would be better than spending the day at the fort, but it was more than that. He enjoyed Mary's company, and her father's fortune seemed to be on the rise.

Jeff awoke Christmas morning to find the weather had cleared after two days of rain, and the temperature had risen so that the day felt more like October than December. Jeff had received a pass from the colonel with a reminder that he should be back by New Year's Day for the dinner that the officers of the regiment were having.

James prepared a hot bath by heating water in a big pot that hung from a contraption in the fireplace. After bathing, James shaved Jeff with a straight razor, though there was little need since, even at his age, the face was still smooth.

Jeff put on his dress uniform that James had pressed with a hot iron, and then he had breakfast before departing the fort. An hour later he arrived on his horse at the Tyler residence. In this frontier county, John Tyler had built the largest log cabin in the countryside.

"Father, he's here," Mary said, her voice shaking with excitement.

John stepped out onto the porch to welcome his guest. He was followed by his wife and three children.

"Welcome, Lieutenant. You had a fine day to travel."

"It was, Sir. Thank you for inviting me."

Mary was pleased with the appearance of this slim young officer who stood before her. He looked impressive in his uniform that had been tailored to fit his six-foot frame. They sat in the parlor, and the housekeeper served them coffee and slices of fruit cake. Afterwards, John and Jeff engaged in a discussion on politics of the day while the ladies excused themselves to finish preparing Christmas dinner.

Though their views on politics were in agreement most of the time, John was a staunch Whig whereas Jeff, influenced by his brother, was a Democrat. John spent some of the conversation speaking of his trade. He imported goods and exported the products of the surrounding region. He maintained a store in a little settlement not far from his home, and he owned some pasture lands nearby where he raised horses. From the contents of the conversation, Jeff realized that this man was looking for a husband for his daughter, Mary, and for a partner who would help him expand his business enterprise. Jeff had the distinct impression that he had settled on him as a likely prospect for both.

"How long is your commitment to the Army?"

"Five years from my graduation at West Point, unless I submit the resignation of my commission sooner."

Jeff had been thinking about resigning his commission even without the prospects of making the man seated across from him a future father-in–law.

The dinner was a glorious array of meats, vegetables, and desserts. It was obvious to all that Mrs. Tyler was pleased with her efforts at impressing the young lieutenant that sat at her table. She looked on him as a good catch for her daughter. He was educated and had an aristocratic manner. They had come from good families back East, and they were determined not to wed their daughter to any of the locals who were lacking in education and sophistication. To accomplish this goal, they were willing to go to great lengths.

That evening at her parents' request, Mary played the piano in the parlor. It was the only such instrument for miles around, and the family took great pride in their possession of it. Mrs. Tyler, an accomplished pianist, had passed on the skill to her daughter.

On December 27, John returned to work at his store, along with the other two daughters that helped out during the school holidays.

"I need to get out of the house," Mary said to Jeff the first day her father returned to work.

They had just finished breakfast and Mrs. Tyler was passing through the dining room. Jeff withheld his reply to see her reaction. Ladies were generally not allowed to be alone with a man without a family member present.

"That is a lovely idea," the mother said. "Why don't you ride over to the stables? I know Jeff is a good judge of horse flesh. Perhaps he could put a good word in for your father with his commanding officer when the army needs to purchase more horses."

"I'll go get dressed in my riding outfit."

Jeff never had an opportunity to reply. He suspected the ladies had already discussed this outside of his presence.

He was surprised when they stepped out onto the porch to see there was no side-saddle on Mary's horse. She saw the expression on his face.

"I was born to ride, and I don't use a side saddle, though I know many who would not approve."

When they were some distance from the house, Mary dug her heels into the side of her horse. Taken by surprise, Jeff wasn't able to catch up with her until she stopped at a small stream and waited for him.

"You are an excellent rider," he said as he reined the horse in beside her.

"You'll learn that I am an independent woman and not just the sweet charming person you have known for the past few months."

She smiled and her face had a devilish expression as the words fell from her lips. They followed the stream until it came to her father's property, then peeled away and headed to the stables that were situated on high ground.

Jeff was impressed with the animals. There were twenty-three of them. He promised Mary to mention the horses to the colonel when he returned to post.

"I know where there is a beautiful stretch of river only a short distance from here," she said. "I'm starving. Let's go by father's store. I'm sure there will be some homemade bread and meats there, and the two of us shall have a picnic."

When they arrived at a cluster of stores and homes, Mary pointed to the one that was her Father's. It was the largest structure in the settlement, and there seemed to be a lot of activity around it, as men were unloading several wagons and carrying merchandise into the store.

"Father," Mary called out as they approached.

He turned and gave them a welcoming gesture.

"We just had a look at your horses Mr. Tyler. They are in great shape. Just the kind of horse flesh the army needs."

"I hope to do business with your colonel in the near future."

"There's always a need for replacements."

They dismounted and strolled into the store, which was built like a warehouse. The two younger girls were sweeping the wooden floor and briefly looked up from their task and giggled at their sister.

The father had already packed them bread and meats and had placed it in a basket, along with a jug of water.

"Have a good time at the bluff," he said.

Mary's face turned red with embarrassment. How could my father have been so stupid? she thought.

As they rode from the settlement, Mary turned to Jeff and said, "It's pretty obvious that my parents have picked you for a son- in law."

Jeff didn't know how to react to such a bold statement, so he just grinned hoping the statement which expected a response would go away, but she followed it up with another statement just as bold.

"I will choose my own husband," she said and then whipped the hindquarters of her horse and took off down the primitive road that led to the bluff. She only slowed down long enough to give Jeff time to catch up just before they reached the river.

The view was gorgeous from the bluff, and they were able to watch a steamer go by. The passengers waved to them from its double decks, and they returned the acknowledgement. When the paddlewheel took the boat upstream, the two spread out a blanket and placed the contents of the basket upon it.

After they had finished eating, Jeff turned his face to Mary who was sitting close to him. She watched his expression, as he looked deep into her eyes. He was a hard man to read, and she had no idea what he was thinking. She felt he would never take the initiative. She needed to heat up the emotion of this very reserved man. She placed her hand on the back of his neck and pulled him toward her until their lips met.

Jeff had wanted to kiss Mary from the moment he had first seen her at the fort. Now it was at last happening. It did not end with a kiss. Soon the two were embracing, and then he laid her down upon the soft pine needles beneath the trees. His hand slipped beneath her blouse. She did not resist and her nipples hardened in such a way that he knew she found pleasure in his touch. While he continued to kiss her, his right hand slipped beneath her riding skirt and pushed up until it found a thick black mound of hair which covered her womanhood. She cried out for him to stop, but he didn't respond until he felt the palms of her hands push him away.

"No Jeff," she said in a firm voice.

He sat up flustered by the experience, and leaned against the trunk of a pine tree.

"You can't do that until we are married, but if you should decide to propose to me, I promise you won't regret it."

Somehow Jeff knew that at least physically, she spoke the truth.

The rest of his stay, Jeff was never able to get Mary alone, and she seemed more distant. This made him desire her even more. He didn't know whether it was just a physical attraction, or if he was truly in love.

* * *

The New Year's Day dinner was restricted to officers. Not even the wives were invited. It was a small group and the liquor flowed freely. Jeff engaged in small talk with his colleagues, but his mind was on Mary until Sidney said, "The colonel's youngest daughter arrived yesterday."

His curiosity aroused, Jeff responded, "What does she look like?"

"A pretty thing. She's small-framed with wavy brown hair, and beautiful hazel eyes that are quite intriguing."

"Maybe she's the one for you," Jeff said.

"Not me. You know I'm engaged to the love of my life. What about you?" Have you committed to Mary?"

"No, but I may very soon. She's quite a strong-willed woman. That's a characteristic I find attractive in members of the opposite sex."

The colonel sent Jeff an invitation to a birthday dinner for his daughter, Sarah, whom everyone called Knoxie. He normally did not wear his dress uniform, but the colonel had mentioned there would be other guests, so James prepared him to look his best. Even his boots were shined. He felt a little nervous. He wondered why. After all, he was thinking of proposing to Mary. Perhaps his nerves were on edge because he had indulged in strong drink the night before. When Knoxie's father introduced them that evening, Jeff discovered what real love was the moment their eyes met. He wanted her, and all thoughts of Mary disappeared as if she had never existed.

Mary arrived at the fort the next day. She could sense something was wrong. All it took was a wave from the colonel's daughter as she passed Jeff on the street to tell Mary he was smitten. She could have struggled to hold onto him, but she knew from the look on his face that he only had eyes for the Taylor girl. Strangely, on the way home Mary felt relieved. She no longer had to wrestle with the issue of whether to accept a proposal from Jeff. She had never been completely sure of how deep her feelings were for him, although he was handsome and a good catch. And had he proposed, it was likely she would have caved in to the pressure from her parents to accept. But she wasn't sure he was the kind of man that could make her happy.

* * *

Knoxie was excited. Jeff had invited her to go riding. In the two weeks since she had arrived at the post, she encountered him several times. She suspected that many of those encounters were not by accident. She knew her father was impressed with this second lieutenant from comments he made during the evening meal when only the family was present; a time when he voiced opinions about officers under his command. If her father suspected she had more than a passing interest in this young man, he would have been unhappy. He had already unsuccessfully tried to discourage her older sister from becoming engaged to a soldier. Not because he disliked the man, but because he was pursuing a military career. Her father had seen the hardships imposed upon his own family as they moved to different frontier forts. Knoxie had heard him on this issue so often that she would never comment to him on any passing interest she might have in an officer.

Not quite as good a horsewoman as Mary, she rode on a side saddle. Knoxie did not have much experience with the four-legged beast upon which she sat. Her riding outfit consisted of a white blouse that was partial covered by a green jacket that matched the skirt that had been hemmed so that it fell only just below the knees for safety's sake. She was content at first to let Jeff do most of the talking, as he described the land and the various tribes that encompassed the area that was the responsibility of the regiment.

"I hope that I'm not boring you," he said.

"Not at all."

Knoxie was particularly fascinated by his description of the Indians. He could speak the language of several nearby tribes. He entertained her by speaking a few of their words and telling her stories of his encounters with them. They stopped by a brook and for the rest of the day, she dominated the conversation with stories of the various posts where they had been stationed, and some of the strange characters she had met along the way. Before they realized it, the sun had begun to go down.

"We need to get back to the fort," Jeff said with some alarm underlying his tone.

Knoxie knew that when he realized how late it was, he was afraid her father might be disturbed with him.

"I'll race you back to the fort," she said.

Jeff could have beaten her easily because he was one of the best horsemen in the region, but he was also a gentleman. When they came within sight of the fort, Knoxie suddenly reined her horse in and stopped. She turned to Jeff who was now beside her.

"I hope we have other opportunities to go riding. I've had such a wonderful day."

"So have I."

Knoxie gave him that smile people had often told her was charming.

After that first day of riding, the two found every excuse they could to be together. She had discovered how attracted he was to her by the poems he would secretly place in her hand as they passed one another in the close confines of the fort. Soon she found that she was not happy when she was apart from him. His infatuation with her was met by her obsession with him. At every opportunity when they could find a spot hidden from the eyes of others, they would kiss in a way that reduced their pent-up passions, if only for the moment. As time went on, she let his hands explore, which only made them crave the company of each other more.

"I've got to speak to your father," he said one day while they were riding. "I want to marry you."

"I want to marry you too, but I've told you how my father feels. He could stop us from seeing each other."

Eventually it could be put off no longer. Knoxie told her mother how she felt, and the two conspired on how to persuade the colonel to consent. A time was agreed upon. The colonel liked to sit on the porch after the evening meal and smoke a cigar while he sipped a glass of whiskey. Jeff would keep a watch on the house and use this opportunity to approach him.

"Good evening, Colonel," Jeff said as he appeared out of the darkness near the porch.

The full moon cast a light upon the figure sitting in the chair. Jeff could smell the cigar that mixed with the scent of whiskey in the air.

"Come up and join me for a drink, Lieutenant."

Jeff took a seat in a chair next to the colonel, and he was immediately handed a jug and a glass. The locally brewed whisky burned his throat. He had to restrain himself not to cough.

The colonel was no fool. He knew why the lieutenant had come, and he dreaded the conversation that was about to follow.

"Colonel, I need to speak with you about a personal matter."

The colonel wanted to cut to the chase, for he personally liked Jeff.

"Is it about Knoxie?"

"You probably realize that we have spent a lot of time together recently."

"It has not escaped my attention."

"I have spoken to her about having a future together."

"What are her feelings on the matter?"

"We are in accord, but before I formally ask her to marry me, so that our engagement can be publicly announced, I wanted to ask your consent."

"I have nothing against you personally, but I don't want my daughter marrying a man in the military. It's too much of a hardship on a woman constantly following her husband and never being able to put down roots."

"Will you consider it?"

"I'll not make a decision tonight, but you have my permission to continue to court her."

At least the answer was not a definite *No*, and he had not forbidden him from seeing her. Now Jeff hoped with Knoxie and Mrs. Taylor's pleas constantly in his ear, the colonel would eventual yield to the inevitable.

While the permission to marry his daughter hung in the balance, Jeff and Taylor had a falling out over a court-martial involving a new recruit. A recently arrived captain had been appointed to serve on the panel in judgment of a private along with Colonel Taylor, Major Smith and Jeff. Under military rules, the captain was to wear his dress uniform, but it had been left in St. Louis. Smith wanted to waive the rule and go forward, for the soldier accused of disobeying a command from his sergeant was being held in the stockade. It was an open facility where the man suffered from the weather. Taylor wanted the accused to be detained, and the trial continued until the captain's uniform arrived. The two men got into a heated argument.

When Jeff spoke and said he would vote with Smith, the colonel took this as a personal affront, and said that no man who had voted with Smith would ever marry his daughter. That evening he forbade his daughter from further contact with Jeff. Things got worse when another officer, who was seduced by Knoxie's charm and wanted to pursue his interest in her, told Taylor that Jeff's actions were intended as a personal insult to him as the commanding officer. Taylor sent an orderly to get Jeff. When he appeared, Taylor upbraided him. He accused Jeff of improper motives. Jeff's face turned beet-red, and he could not withhold his comments when an accusation was made upon his honor. Insulting remarks flowed from his lips before he stormed out of Taylor's presence. Davis went to Sidney's quarters where he asked him to be his second, for Jeff intended to challenge Taylor to a duel. His friend calmed him down by pointing out that he could not kill the father of the woman he loved.

When Knoxie heard of the confrontation, she went to her father in tears. Her distraught state touched his heart. He gave his daughter one ray of hope. He told her that if she still wanted to marry Jeff after two years, he would not stand in their way. The next morning Taylor issued an order directing Jeff to join Colonel Dodge who was being sent to Fort Gibson as soon as the regiment of dragoons authorized by congress could be recruited.

To aide in the recruitment of men for the new regiment, Jeff traveled to Kentucky. The pay was low and the number of men he recruited on this trip amounted to only a dozen, but he was able to spend two weeks in Lexington where he renewed old acquaintances. Unfortunately, there was an outbreak of cholera, and to protect his new troops he had to flee the city.

Jeff marched the men to Jefferson Barracks in St. Louis where the newly appointed commander of the dragoons was already in the process of drilling the raw recruits that had drifted in from the surrounding states. The dragoons were mounted cavalry and this suited Jeff whose father, Samuel, had taught him to be a superb horseman. Upon his arrival, he purchased a dark brown horse from a nearby planter and named him Red Bird, after the tribal leader that had sent his maiden daughter to nurse him back to health when he had been ill with pneumonia.

To the men under his command, Jeff presented a dashing figure in his tailored white drill pants and dress coat; to which he added a pair of expensive fashionable boots. He had the air of command about him. This presence made it easier to drill the troops, and he did so with a passion that was not always appreciated, for no other officer took as great an interest in getting their men trained. Colonel Dodge was so impressed with Jeff that he not only made him his chief of staff, but also put him as second in command of Jefferson Barracks.

In November with the weather already turning cold, Colonel Dodge decided to take his regiment to Fort Gibson which was in an unorganized territory that would later become Oklahoma. It was a three hundred mile journey across Missouri and Arkansas. He made this decision despite the fact that the organization of the regiment was not complete. There were only five companies, and two of them had no horses. Sufficient arms and winter clothing had not arrived, and the colonel planned to start the expedition without these items. Jeff strongly disagreed with the colonel's decision. In several meetings with his commanding officer, he argued against it, his words bordering on insubordination. This revealed a trait he carried in his genes--a natural compassion he had for people, which extended to the men under his command. It would not be the last time he would clash with officers who did not respect the lives of the men serving under them. His actions would be duly noted on his record and act as an impediment to advancement in his military career.

The regiment left in the middle of a rainstorm which lasted for three days. The men's morale, which had been low at the prospects of the journey, sank even further. The second week of the journey the regiment was hit by a blinding snow storm. Food supplies ran low, and the men were reduced to rations of one piece of cornbread a day. Finally after a four-week march, they staggered into Fort Gibson suffering from extreme fatigue and sickness. Jeff, like the others, became ill. His lungs were weak from the prior bout with pneumonia, and he developed a chronic lung infection. He was close to death, and it was only the constant care of James that saved his life once again. Even with James' help, it was spring before he could return to active duty. In the meantime, the colonel replaced Jeff as his chief of staff because of his sharp disagreement with him over the expedition.

Knoxie learned of Jeff's illness from an officer's wife at Fort Crawford whose husband had been on the expedition. She was frantic with worry, which was compounded by the fact she had not received a letter from Jeff in some time. She became so ill that she took to her bed for several days, which caused her parents great concern. While in bed trying to recovery from worry and heartache, she wrote him.

My Dearest Love,
I have just learned that you have been deadly ill. I am in such great distress after having received this information. This news has so saddened me that I think my heart will surely burst if I shall not see you again soon. I have spent hours on my knees in prayer for you, and have fasted in hope that the Almighty will grant you a return of good health. I am counting the days when the two years expire so that we can be married.

Yours forever,
Knoxie

Jeff was despondent about being away from his love. This was not relieved by a correspondence he received from the War Department informing him of his promotion to first lieutenant. He tried to drive thoughts of her from his mind by drilling his men even harder until some were on the point of rebellion. Colonel Dodge realizing a problem was developing, ordered Jeff into the surrounding countryside to find more recruits, for the quota of the regiment had not yet been filled.

At Fort Crawford, Knoxie was lonely. She was also irritated with her father whom she suspected had issued his orders placing Jeff with the dragoon unit as a way to keep him away from her. Now he was aggravating their strained relationship by encouraging a local merchant to court her. If she had to sit down at dinner in their home for one more evening when he was an invited guest, she would probably explode in rage at her father.

Her only consolation was receiving letters intermittently from Jeff. Mail delivery was slow and unreliable. There was such a great lapse of time between when he posted a letter and its arrival. She could tell from the ones she received that others had not been delivered. She suspected her father had intercepted some and withheld them from her. If he thought sending Jeff away would cool her feelings toward him, he had made a mistake. Their separation had only made her realize how much she loved him. Alone that evening in her bedroom, she read for the tenth time the correspondence which had arrived that day.

My Dearest Knoxie,
Words cannot express the heartache I feel being separated from you. The days are long and the nights even longer without the pleasure of your company. Oh, how I long to hold you in my arms and speak the words of our favorite ballad, "The Fairy Belles," or even better, hear you play the tune as you do so well on the piano. I am terrified that your feeling toward me will change and another will win your heart while we are separated by the great distance of geography and of time. My heart belongs to you through eternity.

Love always,
Jeff

She sat at her writing desk in the bedroom and composed a response.

Jeff,
You need not worry. Neither time nor distance will change my love for you. Do not concern yourself about others. No other man shall win my heart. We shall be married since my father has given me his word that he will not prevent it if I still feel towards you in two years as I do now.

The wait is such a dreadful experience. What a waste of our lives that we must delay so long because my father is so determined to keep us apart. He is a stubborn man, but I love him. To be caught between two people you love is a situation I have never had to endure before. But endure it I shall, and we will marry when the two years have passed, even if it is without my Father's blessings.

My mother sends her love and has great sympathy for our situation.

My heart is yours forever,
Knoxie

* * *

General Leavenworth was in charge of Fort Gibson, and that spring he decided to send the company under Jeff's command to provide protection for laborers who were in the process of constructing Fort Jackson on a site that lay twenty miles away. With his health returned, Jeff was glad for the new orders. His melancholy disappeared as he took advantage of the diversion.

On the journey to the site, Jeff was almost killed when he was thrown by his horse after coming upon a bear. He was able to retrieve his musket just in time and fired into its heart as it stood on its hind legs and hovered over him. When the animal fell, Jeff had just enough time to roll away to avoid being crushed.

As a diversion from the boredom at the construction camp, Jeff rode over to an Indian village that lay to the south and spent the day with Sam Houston, who had taken an Indian wife after he had left the governor-ship of Tennessee. He arrived early in the morning and found Houston drinking whisky. All day Houston entertained him with stories until the former governor passed out.

Jeff's men showed signs of restlessness for action, so he was glad when an order arrived from General Leavenworth to join him on an expedition to establish contact with the Pawnee in the south-central plains. Besides the objectives of signing a peace treaty and trade agreements, they were sent to investigate a report that had reached Fort Gibson of two white captives living with the tribe. The army was to try to secure their release.

The expedition was composed of five hundred men. The inefficiency of the War Department was visibly apparent. One of the companies had just arrived a few days earlier from Jefferson Barracks, and was clothed in their winter uniforms. They suffered greatly from the heat. The rations issued were completely inadequate for the time it would take the men to reach their objective. Only a few days out, the officers were hunting buffalo to supply food to their men. The meat was lean and tough to eat. Even James complained that when he tried to soften the meat by making a stew, it was impossible to do so without flour.

During one of the hunts, the general was injured by a buffalo and although he lingered for a few days, he finally succumbed. Colonel Dodge took command. He was a man whose leadership abilities were already held in low regards by both the officers and the enlisted men. Their woes continued as the water ran out before they found a stream. In a weakened state, the men stumbled into a Pawnee village. They had lost one hundred men from dysentery, hunger, and exhaustion. Two weeks later when the survivors regained a measure of their health, the Pawnee chiefs arrived. After two days of meetings, a treaty was signed.

Before the infantrymen departed, a young white child was delivered to them. He was burned by the sun to a crisp brown, and he looked like the other Indian children. It was only by bribing him with sweets that they were able to get him to go with them, for he was friends with the children that surrounded him. He refused at first to speak English, but instead he spoke the language of the Pawnee. This changed after he was in their company for a few days. Soon he would be reunited with the farm family from whence he was taken during a raid. The other white child reported among them had been his sister. The Pawnee could not surrender her, because she had already been sold to another tribe as a slave, so they had to depart without her.

The purpose of the expedition having been concluded, Colonel Dodge led the men back to Fort Gibson where he assumed command until the War Department could send a replacement. By that point, the colonel's antagonism toward Jeff had grown so great that he couldn't stand the sight of him. Jeff felt the same way toward the colonel and took every opportunity to avoid him. So when orders were sent to construct barracks at Fort Jones, Colonel Dodge dispatched a company under Captain Mason to supervise the work and assigned Jeff to the company. He was glad to go, but little did he realize at the time that the captain would turn out to be as bad a commanding officer as the colonel.

During his stay at Gibson, Jeff had received a constant stream of letters from his sister-in-law, Eliza. In her own immature way she wanted to befriend him, because she realized there was no family member closer to Joseph. It was obvious from every letter she wrote, she desperately wanted to please her husband. She was like a child trying to please her father. He saw only problems in the future as Eliza grew up and Joseph grew old. How could this marriage ever work? His brother had one of the most brilliant minds in the South, and she was just a girl whose mother had operated a bakery in New Orleans. Perhaps they loved one another. Love of a woman was a concept he could understand now that he had met Knoxie.

Captain Mason lacked the people skills necessary to command men. He did not get along with his officers, though Jeff was the only one to stand his ground when the man became overbearing. The final straw came during a rainstorm. Jeff, who was suffering from malaria coupled with lung congestion, failed to appear for roll call. Captain Mason sent an orderly to fetch him.

"Why were you absent from roll call?" the captain asked.

"Because I was in my tent. When there is rain, regulations allow for the roll call to be taken in the tent by the chief of squads."

Jeff's reply was in a tone not proper when answering a superior officer, but he had no respect for the man. The tone made Mason bristle, as Jeff knew it would.

"You know my standing verbal order is for all officers to attend roll call in the presence of their respective company."

Jeff turned around and walked off in a manner that Mason found disrespectful. Immediately he ordered him to turn around and report back to him. When Jeff complied, Mason upbraided him.

"You are under arrest. Now report to your quarters and remain there until further orders."

At this particular moment Jeff's company marched by, and everything that was transpiring could be overheard by the men. He felt humiliated.

"Now are you done with me?" he asked.

Mason repeated his order once again.

"You are placed under arrest and confined to your quarters."

Jeff did an about-face and marched back to his tent. Inside he was seething with anger. A few minutes later a courier arrived with a letter for him. It was from his mother. His sister Matilda had died.

Captain Mason was not one to allow any resistance to his authority. He filed charges against Jeff, for insubordination, violation of orders, and actions unbecoming an officer. Those higher up in command encouraged the captain to drop the matter which they thought sprung from pettiness. Mason refused, so the matter proceeded to trial. Jeff, who had spent considerable time reading law over the years, decided to represent himself though he had several officers who offered their services.

The military court was put in the uncomfortable position of considering the case of a superior officer versus an inferior officer under his command. The outcome normally would have been a forgone conclusion, but the facts in favor of Mason were weak, and Jeff's arguments were logical and well presented. Still, the court's officers had to worry about the implications of their decision on the command structure. When the verdict was returned, they found Jeff guilty of having failed to report for roll call, but not of being disrespectful or insubordinate. They attached no criminality to his actions, and further found his conduct was not subversive of good order or military discipline. It would appear to be a victory for Jeff, but it stung his pride that they found he had disobeyed an order. Eleven days later he sent his letter of resignation to the new commander at Fort Gibson, General Arbuckle. He asked him to hold it for six weeks before he forwarded it to the War Department in Washington.

The verdict brought Jeff to a decision, for which there were many reasons. He still hoped to get Colonel Taylor's blessing to marry his daughter if he left the army. He was also fed up with the incompetence he had to deal with from commandeering officers who had no respect for the common soldier. Then there was the issue of how to find a way to accumulate wealth if he was going to carrying out his dream of entering the ruling hierarchy. He wrote a letter to his beloved, holding secret the numerous other reasons for submitting his resignation and setting forth only the one that would endear him to her.

My Darling Knoxie,
I have submitted my resignation from the Army. I am hopeful the Secretary of War will accept it. This should gain your father's approval for us to marry, for I know how much you desire his blessing.

You are in my heart and thoughts.

Yours forever,
Jeff

Obtaining a leave of absence, he departed for Mississippi after writing to Joseph a full account of what had occurred and explaining in detail all the reasons for his decision to resign his commission in the army.

Although Eliza had written Jeff many letters while he was away, she had received very few responses. Now she was determined to win his favor when he arrived at *Hurricane,* because she knew how close her husband was to this brother. She worked the house slaves hard to get the home prepared for his visit. She also planned to have a social gathering with available young ladies so Jeff might meet them. But she changed her mind when she received a letter from Knoxie.

Dear Eliza,

I have taken the liberty of writing you though we have never met. Jeff has proposed marriage, and I have decided to accept even if my actions are over the objection of my father. I do not know when this event will occur, but since Jeff is leaving the army, I see no point in any long delay in this matter.

Jeff is very close to your husband, and I believe he will want to return to the Natchez area. I shall encourage him in this matter, because I think it is very important to him. Since we are about the same age, I hope we shall become close friends, and I shall look to you as one would a sister and seek your guidance in matters that are important to the both of us.

I have not written a letter to Jeff recently because I know he has left Fort Gibson and cannot be sure where to post it, but I am sure he is traveling to Hurricane. When you see him, please let him know that with my parents' consent I am going to stay with my Aunt Elizabeth Taylor. She is my father's sister and lives on her plantation, Beechland, near Louisville, Kentucky. My aunt is favorably inclined to have Jeff visit us there, and my mother is aware of our unofficial engagement. My father is still opposed though he placed me on the steamer knowing my plans when I get to Louisville. Even my tears as we parted did not move him to support my actions.

Your future sister,
Knoxie

When Joseph received a letter from Jeff, he wasn't surprised by its contents. He had already reached the conclusion from Jeff's last visit that his brother wasn't going to make the military a career. The numerous correspondences from his brother had also implied that Jeff would eventually marry Sarah Knox. With these two factors in mind, Joseph set about a course of action that he hoped would result in his brother making a permanent home at Davis Bend. He had already gathered those he loved either at *Hurricane* or within easy reach of it. The only one missing was Jeff. His permanent presence would complete the circle. In hopes that his plan would be successful, he ordered his slaves to cut the trees on a tract of land adjacent to the boundaries of his property near *Hurricane*. Although he had sold a few parcels of land to others he found suitable as neighbors, he had retained this one tract in the hope that Jeff might one day return. He now looked forwarded to that prospect coming to fruition.

When Jeff and James got off the steamer at Davis Bend, Joseph stood there waiting. He did not try to hide his joy but rushed forth and embraced them. The three men rode to *Hurricane* on horses which Joseph had brought with him. When they arrived, the Davis clan was waiting on the veranda. Even his mother, who was in declining health, had traveled from Rosemont to welcome him. They cheered Jeff like a returning hero. The house slaves and many of those that worked in the fields were also present to welcome their master's brother.

In the crowd of slaves was a fifteen-year-old girl who watched with great interest as James dismounted. She was more than a cursory onlooker. Julia Ann was twelve years old when James left home with Jeff, and despite her age at that time, she had set her cap for him. Though she had offers from other men on the plantation, she had resisted them. Her virginity remained intact, and she intended to keep it that way until she could capture James' attention. She had set her sights high, but that was not an unusual trait in her family. Her father was Benjamin Montgomery, and she had been raised in an educated household where hard work, education, and family were the three central values taught by her parents. Her bloodlines, like James, held no taint from those who considered themselves the master race, and she took pride in her complete blackness.

After breakfast the next morning with the entire family, Jeff and Joseph went riding across the plantation. Joseph pointed out with pride how he was a diversified farmer. Unlike his neighbors, he was not totally dependent on cotton. They rode past fruit orchards, and acres dedicated to the production of corn. There were also abundant pasture lands with a variety of livestock. As they rode, Joseph suggested that he would help Jeff secure some land if he remained resolute on his decision to leave the army. That way he explained, Jeff could make a new career as a planter, which would make him financially independent.

"There is an undeveloped section of land I want you to see," Joseph said.

They followed what in earlier times had been an Indian trail which the tribes had used as a trade route from the interior to the Mississippi. The process was slow and took an hour for them to arrive there, even though it was less than two miles from *Hurricane*. The Indian trail ended in a clump of oaks. Much to Jeff's surprise, on the other side of them were several acres that had been cleared of trees. With the removal of the shade that the forest had provided, the land had become densely covered with cane and briers.

"This tract contains 800 acres," Joseph said. "I started cutting the trees from this portion right after your last visit. Our conversation during that time led me to believe that you might leave the military. If you still have a desire to become a planter as you have indicated in the past, this would be a good site. It is near the river and the land is fertile."

"Joseph, I'm without resources."

"I'll give you the entire tract."

"I can't accept that. Let me give you a mortgage on the property and pay you back when I can."

"No, I'll hold the title until you get established. Then I'll convey it in satisfaction of any claim you may have against our father's estate and against any claim upon our mother's property."

"That is very generous of you."

"I will do whatever is necessary to have you close by. You are not only my brother but also my closest friend and confidant."

"That expresses my feeling as well."

And it was true. No two men could have been closer than Jeff and his brother, Joseph.

Any question in Jeff's mind about not leaving the army was settled when he received word that the ruling in the court-martial had been upheld by General Gaines on appeal. When Jeff did not return to his post past the April 20th leave, General Arbuckle sent Jeff's resignation to higher authority. It was accepted by the War Department in Washington, and a directive was issued allowing Jeff to resign his commission effective June 30th, 1835. This closed a chapter in Jeff's life, and he looked forward to turning the page by marrying Knoxie and establishing himself as a planter.

THE PLANTER

When Jeff left Fort Gibson, he did not know that Knoxie had gone to live with her aunt near Louisville. When Jeff received this information from Eliza at *Hurricane,* he was ecstatic and immediately made plans to visit her.

Upon the news that the army would soon release him, Jeff set out for Louisville during the latter weeks of May. Knoxie and he had corresponded about their wedding and their plans afterwards. She was anxious to start a new life with him as soon as possible and suggested June 17th for their wedding.

Knoxie composed a letter to her mother informing her of the wedding date and their plans to immediately thereafter leave for *Brierfield,* a name Jeff had given his plantation. In earlier letters, she had led her mother to believe they would wait until the sickness season was over before traveling to Mississippi. The couple's plans changed however, when Jeff assured her the area was healthy. Her mother responded quickly with a letter of concern and a sum of money from her father. They were worried they might never see their daughter again.

In the early afternoon, Knoxie wore her best bonnet and traveling dress. In the parlor of Beechland, they exchanged their vows, surrounded by her aunt and a few kinsmen from the area. Afterwards they left for Davis Bend aboard the steamboat, *Magnolia.*

Their arrival at *Hurricane* was a grand affair. Not only kinsmen and slaves but also the local community turned out to welcome the new couple. Though Joseph's house was not the luxurious kind a person would find in such places as Charleston or New Orleans, it was a fine home by Knoxie's standards, which were set by the housing found on frontier posts. The social event of their coming was celebrated for three days with many of the guests spending the nights. Jeff and Joseph were pleased. They saw that people found Knoxie to be refined and intelligent. Her outgoing personality was a hit. And Eliza loved her, if for no other reason than the fact that she treated her with the respect one should receive as the lady of the house.

Jeff was glad when the coach arrived to take the two to their cottage in Warrenton, where they would spend a few weeks. Then the couple would return to live at *Hurricane* while Jeff constructed a cottage at *Brierfield.* This would be their temporary residence until Jeff built a proper planter's mansion.

As the coach made its way to Warrenton, Jeff and Knoxie talked, laughed, and flirted with one another. Underneath this gaiety, there was a repressed sexual tension. With so many guests, the two had not shared the same bedroom. Knoxie had shared a bed with three other ladies and Jeff had shared a bed with two cousins. So even though they had been married for several days, this was to be their wedding night, for they had not had the opportunity to consummate their marriage.

The white cottage was a one story structure with five rooms. It was located on a side street one block from the business district. A beautiful manicured yard provided a welcome to any visitor. Joseph had secured the use of it from a friend who lived in Vicksburg and only stayed there when he wanted to spend time away from hustle and bustle of his mercantile business.

"It's so lovely," Knoxie said, when the coach pulled up outside.

After stepping from the coach onto a millstone that was appropriately placed to prevent a lady from getting mud on her shoes after a rainstorm, she hurried up the walkway anxious to see what their living quarters looked like inside. As she approached the front door, a young Negress appeared.

"Good morning Ma'am. I'm Lizzie, the cook and housekeeper."

Knoxie gave her a smile and walked into the front room while Jeff was busy helping the coachman with the trunks. The place had been freshly painted and the windows were opened to carry the offensive smell outside.

"I lives with my husband and three children over the dry good store on Main Street. We belongs to the owner of the store, Mr. Hatchel, but he rents out my services to the gentleman who owns this house. Mr. Hatchel says, Lizzie, you takes good care of the house while those newlyweds are there, and be sure and fix the noon day meal every day."

"Thanks," Knoxie said. "That will be a great help."

Knoxie liked this black woman who had such a friendly disposition. If she turned out to be a good cook, maybe she could use the money her father sent her as a wedding present to buy this woman from her owner. Of course, Jeff would insist on purchasing the entire family. She already knew how her husband felt about dividing families. He was too compassionate a person ever to do that. That was one of the characteristics she admired in him.

The kitchen was filled with the smells of chicken baking. Knoxie 's curiosity had her looking into every pot. She found butterbeans, fresh tomatoes, and rice already cooked. The food was sitting on a warmer above hot coals.

"Jeff," she said as they explored the rooms which were fully furnished, "isn't this wonderful. I'd be happy to stay forever."

"And so would I," he replied.

Though he knew after a few days, he would be antsy to return to *Hurricane* and begin work on his land and cottage.

The pair took a stroll about town and walked the streets of the residential area. Neither of which took a very long time. When they arrived back at the house, they excused Lizzie until the next morning and went to work unloading their personal possessions from the four wooden trunks. As darkness settled upon the cottage, Knoxie and Jeff set in the dining room for a romantic first dinner. Jeff located some candles and opened the small wine case that Joseph had given him. It contained three reds of ancient vintage. The first two they opened turned out to be bad, but the third was like something from heaven. They drank it and consumed food left over from the noon day meal. Neither ate much food, for both were excited about sharing a bed for the first time. Knoxie was the more nervous of the two, because she had no experience. Jeff was more excited than nervous since he was not a virgin, and he had the advantage that the women he had slept with were experienced in lovemaking.

Knoxie bathed with water from a wash basin and then slipped on a beautiful night gown her aunt's seamstress had made for this special occasion. Opening a bottle of vanilla extract, she put a touch behind each ear-lobe and on the cleavage between her breasts. Then she slipped beneath the covers and waited for Jeff who was out on the porch giving her time to prepare.

When Jeff entered the room, he saw the outline of her face from the flickering light of a candle that Knoxie had placed on a piece of furniture beside the bed. He undressed and in a naked state quickly wiped the sweat from his body, using a damp cloth that Knoxie had left beside the basin. After slipping beneath the covers, he pulled her toward him.

"I love you," she whispered in his ear.

Deeply touched by her sincerity and the softness of her voice, he pulled her even tighter against his chest for a moment, then he pressed his lips upon hers. They remained in that position for some time, as he felt her small frame shiver against his body.

Knoxie felt his hands upon her small breasts. The nipples that set upon these little mounds of flesh seemed to have a mind of their own as they stiffened and then swelled under his touch. Soon his right hand was beneath her nightgown. She soon recognized it as a barrier between them.

"Jeff, help me take this off."

Together they removed it. Jeff did not rush his movement, but was gentle with his bride as his lips discovered her nipples, and his hand moved over her womanhood. When he felt she was ready, he mounted her. As he entered, she gave a short cry of pain, and then began to move in rhythm with him in a way that had existed since the beginning of time. Afterward, they held one another tight. Jeff had never known such happiness as he held Knoxie in his arms. For the first time, his life felt complete.

The days spent in Warrenton would always be remembered as one of the best times of his life, but the duties of the plantation called. With regrets, they loaded their belongings into a coach and returned to *Hurricane*. They were assigned a large upstairs bedroom at the end of a hallway so they could have some privacy. The room had sparse furniture, but it did contain a bed, writing desk, and two padded chairs. Three large windows provided substantial light and a cheerful atmosphere. In the evenings when they retired, Eliza made sure there were enough candles to provide light sufficient for them to read. Books were easily accessed from Joseph's library, which had the largest private collection of books in the cotton states.

* * *

Joseph was pleased with the way Jeff attacked the challenge posed by the treeless portion of the land covered by a healthy growth of wild cane and briers. Seeing his industry, he promised Jeff he would add another thousand acres to the tract now called *Brierfield* Plantation. But he still was hesitant about putting the title into Jeff's name, because he felt his brother was too unsettled about the course of his life. He could very well decide to go back into the army or even perhaps seek his fortune in Texas. The last thing he wanted was to give Jeff the option of selling the land to another. The thoughts of a stranger owning property so close to *Hurricane* did not sit well with him, and he was never going to allow this to happen.

Seeing the slow progress Jeff and James were making against the awesome task confronting them, Joseph sent some slaves to help get the land ready to plant cotton. He soon realized this would not work since it interfered with his own operation. There was only one possible alternative. Jeff must have more laborers. He would give his brother a loan, and hope he would stay *at Brierfield* long enough to pay him back. So Joseph and Jeff went to Natchez on board the *Magnolia* steamboat. Jeff purchased ten Negroes on his brother's line of credit and took them aboard the steamer.

A cabin that Joseph had built in 1832 on land that now constituted *Brierfield* served as a place for James to live. He oversaw the construction of cabins for the new slaves. They were from different parts of the South. Joseph had advised Jeff it would be best if the ten slaves had no bonding between them before they reached *Brierfield*. That could mean trouble. Their new lives should begin here with no shared memories. All were young and strong. Their ages ranged from sixteen to twenty. Until the construction of their cabins was completed, they still had to be housed among the slaves at *Hurricane*. But there was an advantage to this temporary arrangement. In this way they would become acclimated to the society that existed at Davis Bend, and would quickly realize the treatment here was based on kindness and a structure of fairness, as long as assigned tasks were completed.

The thick cane and briers proved too dense to cut or uproot, so they burned them instead. Jeff worked alongside James and the ten slaves digging shallow holes in the earth into which they placed the cotton seed. The slaves were still housed on Joseph's plantation. So some days were spent cutting trees in the surrounding forest to build slave cabins, as well as outbuildings for horses, livestock, and farm implements.

* * *

James heard a knock on his cabin door. When he opened it, a slave girl stood there holding a basket of food. No one else was around on the place since it was Sunday. James had decided not to attend services with Jeff at the Episcopal Church in Natchez, as he normally did because he was too weary from work. There was a second reason, however. He wanted to spend some time alone, but the company of an attractive female quickly drove away the desire for solitude.

"I thought you might like some good home cooking. You must get tired of fixing your own grub."

She pulled back the red checkered cloth that covered the contents of the basket she was carrying. Several pieces of fried chicken and some biscuits came into view.

"This will go good with the mess of collard greens and yams I just finished cooking, girl."

"I'm not a girl," she said with defiance in her voice.

She quickly replaced the angry scowl that had crossed her face with the sweet smile of an angel.

James noticed her English was impeccable, and he quickly guessed whose family she belonged to.

"What's your name?"

"Julia Ann Montgomery."

She was the youngest daughter of Ben Montgomery, who had become the business manager of *Hurricane* and an entrepreneur in his own right with Joseph's blessing. He operated a store of his own at the dock at Davis Bend where he sold produce to passing boats.

"I thought so," he said as his mind raced back over the years. "I remember you now. You were a scrawny little thing when I left *Hurricane* with Mr. Jeff the first time."

"I'm not scrawny now," she said as she gave him the basket.

After that comment, Julia Ann placed a hand on her hip and braced her body backward so that her well-developed breasts were pushed forward against the thin material of her blouse.

"Aren't you going to invite me in?"

* * *

After the cotton-seeds were planted, and work was completed on the slave's quarters, Jeff turned his attention to building a spacious cottage for Knoxie. He fancied himself an architect. He had observed the structure of not only the homes in the area, but also remembered the ones he had seen in his travels. Comfort more than style was his central aim.

At night by candle light in the bedroom they shared at *Hurricane*, he would show Knoxie his drawings. She was caught up in his excitement, and they both hoped when the cotton was harvested in the fall that construction could commence.

"Come look out the window," Jeff said one morning, as he entered the bedroom.

"What is it Jeff?" she asked, as she got out of the bed and went toward the window, wondering why he seemed so excited.

Below, James was holding the reins of a colt.

"What a beautiful animal."

"It's for you."

"What's the special occasion?" she asked with a puzzled look on her face.

"That I'm in love."

She went over and placed herself in his arms.

"No one could have a finer man then you," she said.

After receiving another correspondence from her mother, who again expressed her concern about Knoxie staying near the river in Mississippi during the sickness season, she penned a reply saying that she need not worry, the area was quite healthy.

* * *

James was getting married. The courtship had happened so quickly that Jeff was taken by complete surprise when James came to him one evening requesting his permission to marry.

"Have you spoken to Joseph? She belongs to him."

"Mr. Joseph has consented on condition that you approve."

The small wedding was held at the Episcopal Church in Natchez. Strange though it would sound to later generations, slaves frequently sat with their master's family at church on Sunday, and house slaves often married in the church. Just before the wedding, James purchased his Julia Ann from Joseph with money he had saved. Under army regulations, officers were entitled to have one servant who received pay and rations. With Jeff's approval, James had saved his pay. When they stood before the minister, James owned her, but no one saw the twisted irony of the situation.

Weeks after James' wedding, Knoxie rode out to *Brierfield* to see what progress was being made on finishing the cottage. When Jeff saw her break through the tree line and gallop toward him, he was alarmed. The place was covered with swarms of mosquitoes from heavy rains that had fallen over the last few days. He told her to go to James's house and he would join her shortly.

Julia Ann offered Knoxie a chair on the porch and fixed tea for her to drink while she waited for Jeff to finish the day's work so they could ride back together to *Hurricane*.

"I see you are expecting," Knoxie said.

"I didn't know it showed."

"Only in the radiant expression on your face."

Knoxie became ill that night at *Hurricane* and by morning she had a high fever. As her condition worsened, Jeff also fell ill. The only other white person on the plantation was the overseer. Joseph had left the day after James' wedding and had taken his family with him to Maine to avoid the fever season. Jeff decided the two would be better off at Locust Grove, where his sister, Anna, could take care of them. By the time a small boat was readied for the journey, Knoxie was so ill, she had to be taken down to the dock on a litter. Jeff was able to board on his own though he was deathly pale and shook uncontrollably while walking alongside his wife and holding a parasol to shield her from the sun.

They both lapsed into delirium during the journey and had to be taken from the boat on a litter into Anna's home. After the two were placed in separate rooms off a hallway, Anna sent for a doctor. When he arrived he gave Anna little hope that either would survive. He gave her some herbal powder to dispense and directed her on the portions and times she should dispense it.

On Sept. 15, during a brief period of consciousness, Jeff heard his wife's voice singing a song they both loved, "Fairy Bells." It took all his strength to struggle from his bed and stagger down the hallway to her room. Just as he reached it, the voice stopped. Her body lay motionless. He set on the bed and took her in his arms and cried.

When Anna heard a loud wailing, she rushed to Knoxie's room. At first, Jeff refused to release Knoxie's body. When he finally did, Anna and a house slave helped him down the hallway to his bed. The next morning Jeff, still in a fevered state, demanded that the funeral be conducted in his room, for he was too ill to leave the bed. Afterwards, she was buried in the family plot at Locust Grove. She was only twenty-one, and the couple had been married less than four months.

During the next six weeks Jeff teetered between life and death, but under Anna's constant care, he slowly began to improve. When he was finally able to sit on the porch, he was emaciated. Spasms of coughing frequently racked his body. In late October, James carried Jeff in his arms to the boat landing, where he was placed on a steam boat that took him to *Hurricane.*

On the plantation, Jeff remained bedridden for another month. At least he had the comfort of being surrounded by many loved ones. Few in the household thought he would survive. Then he began to recover. However, his left eye, which had given him trouble since he fell ill with pneumonia during the winter spent cutting lumber on the Yellow River, continued to give him intermittent problems. Even when he was able to walk about the plantation, he was partially blind. Eventually his sight returned, though it would cause him pain at times for the rest of his life.

* * *

Although the winters in Mississippi were mild, Joseph convinced Jeff to spend it in a warm climate knowing that his brother's health was still fragile, and that he was suffering from a deep depression. In early December, Jeff boarded a steamboat for New Orleans with James. Several days after they arrived in that bustling city, the two boarded a ship for Havana. During the week's voyage to Cuba, James had Jeff's cot placed on deck. The fresh air, coupled with shock treatments that James provided by pouring buckets of cold sea water over him improved his mental health.

Entering Havana's harbor, they were presented with the beautiful sight of pink and white stucco buildings. They checked into the Plaza Hotel. While in the city, Jeff did not reach out to the local population. Instead, he used this time to recover his physical and mental health by taking solitary walks about the city and on the beaches. While there, he continued his interest in sketching and frequently used as his subjects the people he observed while he sat drinking coffee at the cafes that dotted the city. Other things attracted his interest, such as the fortifications that lined the harbor and the constant parading of troops. The military authorities became suspicious and took him before the local commander. Jeff was informed that if he continued to sketch the forts and troops that he would be tried as a spy. His sketchbooks were confiscated. James was also questioned. Only his vivid description of the plight that brought his master to Havana convinced the military commander to release Jeff from the dungeon where he was being held. The two decided it best to depart the island before the authorities had a change of heart. Luckily, a ship was leaving in two days for New Orleans.

In March 1836, their ship arrived in New Orleans. Several days later they took a steamship up the Mississippi to *Hurricane*. For the next two years, Jeff lived at Joseph's home and buried himself in the work at *Brierfield* trying to establish it as a working plantation. Though he never told anyone, except James, Jeff's grief was made deeper because he blamed himself for bringing Knoxie to Mississippi at the height of the sickness season. At the time of his marriage, he desperately wanted to begin his new life as a planter and have Knoxie beside him. To delay would have meant not planting his cotton for another season. He did not want to leave her in Kentucky while he returned to oversee the planting. He had already been denied her company for two years. Knoxie had been hesitant, but she loved him and therefore had relied on his word that it would be safe. He felt his impatience had resulted in her death. It was a terrible burden to carry, but he cringed at the very idea of getting emotional support by confessing this information. No one but James knew the guilt he carried. The rest of his life there would be a permanent scar on his conscience.

The trials and tribulations Jeff had suffered made him grow even closer to Joseph, and their relationship became more like father and son. He was a changed man. His mind was now like a clean slate. Onto it Joseph poured his knowledge of things and his philosophy of life. Every evening they discussed a broad range of topics from the proper treatment of slaves to political events in America and Europe. Jeff also buried himself in reading books from his brother's extensive library. Among the writings he studied were the works of Virgil, Milton, Byron, and Burns, as well as the novels of Walters Scott, and James Fennimore Cooper. He studied Shakespeare and read poetry. He digested The Federalist papers, the reports of the Congressional debates, and the Virginia and Kentucky Resolutions of 1798 and 1799. These resolutions supported Thomas Jefferson's theory that a state might set aside laws of the federal government that it found objectionable. It was during this period that Jeff's views on the Constitution were formed on an intellectual basis, and he would never veer from that foundation despite the costs it would later create for him personally, to his people, and to the nation he loved.

During this period of grief he read every page of the Bible for the first time. He particularly liked the Songs of Solomon and the Book of Job, though he never turned to organized religion for comfort. Instead, he buried his grief in work and reading. He was too proud to seek emotional support from those around him. He developed a stoical will and self-control that was a characteristic of his father, a man who had spent his life behind a façade, only occasionally allowing his deeper feelings to be seen by others. For the rest of his life, Jeff would cultivate a dignified reserve to hide the turmoil he felt inside.

* * *

Joseph was an enlightened person for the times. He had read the works of the famous utopian Robert Owens and had been blessed by a two-day encounter with him on a stagecoach ride while traveling in the Northern States.

In every respect *Hurricane* was a wonderfully humane experience in the operation of an enterprise, except that the workers on the plantation were slaves. It was a self-sufficient community, where no one lacked the necessary material things of life.

"I wish there was a way to free them without upending the social order," he said to Jeff one evening in the library.

"At this period of our history, I don't see an easy way to accomplish that," Jeff said.

"Yes, it would be very difficult. A few years ago while you were at West Point, I contributed to an organization raising money to purchase their freedom and transport them back to Africa. It had quite a large following throughout the South and even had many adherents here in Mississippi. The funds dried up when the abolitionists started calling Southerners immoral and advocating that our slaves rise up and slay us."

The two brothers never accepted the concept that Negroes were inferior as a race, and they foresaw that sometime in the future they would be freed, but neither did they believe that all Negroes were equal any more than they believed all white man were equal. When they observed Negroes who were intellectually alert, they encouraged them to read and granted them the use of books. All of which was extraordinary for the times.

Jeff adopted Joseph's philosophy of slave management and implemented it at *Brierfield*. This policy made a better life for them and a prosperous living for him. He also implemented Joseph's methods when a slave was accused of wrong doing. He impaneled a jury of slaves and let the accused be tried by a jury of peers. Slaves were never beaten at *Hurricane* or *Brierfield*, nor were they sold. Both brothers thought of them as an extension of their family, though they frequently viewed them as children just as they did their spouses.

Not whipping his slaves was something Jeff found easy to do because of his aversion to physical punishment. He always believed alternative methods were better. His closeness to James had made it easy for him to treat individuals with respect, even if that person was a slave. For the duration of his life when one of his slaves was accused of some wrong doing, his standard response would be, "I will ask him to give me his account of it." Then he would ask the accused to give his side of the story. Like his brother, Jeff allowed his slaves free access to his chickens, the corn cribs, and fruit trees. They were allowed to raise produce and sell it, as well as chickens, to ships that stopped at Davis Bend.

* * *

In many ways, Knoxie's death was a watershed in Jeff's life and permanently influenced his future course of conduct. After this traumatic experience, he never regained his appetite and always had a gaunt look. His disinterest in food was to the extent that when he purchased a Natchez slave girl who was auctioned as trained in the kitchen, he never complained when it became obvious that she had never cooked before. The first morning she forgot to cook him breakfast, and he satisfied himself with a glass of milk. When it was time for the evening meal, she had prepared nothing. Upon realizing this he said, "Don't trouble yourself. It is late, just try to have breakfast tomorrow." In the end he only required her to be sure that he had at least some cornpone or hoecake with any meal she prepared.

Death of any kind disturbed Jeff in the aftermath of what had been taken away from him. He no longer loved to roam the woods and hunt small game with his rifle. Eventually, he prohibited anyone from shooting wild animals on his plantation, except for his slaves who were allowed to kill game to supply the plantation with fresh meat. During this period of his life he also gave up strong drink. His stomach would not tolerate it anymore.

The Jefferson Davis that existed before Knoxie's death, a man who loved to party, dance, and flirt with the opposite sex no longer existed. The young cadet who was exuberant, unruly, and mischievous had disappeared except in relationship with his immediate family and close friends. Later in his life this reserved manner would be described by his enemies as cold. Some of his earlier characteristics however remained. He was still one who felt empathy with those who were under the authority of others, and he still resented those in authority who tried to direct his course. He also retained an excessive sense of honor and tended to see everything as right or wrong. He rarely saw anything as a gray area. He retained a deep reserve of discipline, and a capacity to apply all his faculties toward a goal. These traits often conflicted with a streak of indecision when he faced matters involving his career.

During the next two years, Jeff rarely left Davis Bend. He spent his time focused on improving his plantation and reading. James acted as the overseer, and he was able to get the other slaves to produce a full day's work.

The monotony of farming was broken when the owner of an adjoining tract of land started to cut a wide canal on his property's border with *Hurricane*. If it were allowed to be completed, it would create a tributary for the waters from the Mississippi to flow through and leave the lands owned by Jeff and Joseph an island.

"I've filed papers in the equity court asking for a temporary injunction to stop the digging until this matter can be heard on the merits," Joseph said to Jeff as they sat in the library discussing the matter.

"I went and observed that the number of laborers has tripled. They have brought in about fifty Irish laborers to supplement the forty Negroes," Jeff said.

"Probably because he was served with the complaint last week. I'm sure his aim is to complete the canal before the case can be heard."

"Is that possible?" Jeff asked.

"I'm afraid so," Joseph said. "The next term of court is two months away. If the canal is finished, the court will see no need to issue a temporary injunction. By the time the matter is heard on the merits, the tributary he will have created will be irreversible."

The two men pondered what could be done.

"I'm an officer of the court and prefer the legal route whenever possible, but in this situation that is not a viable option. We must take the law into our own hands."

"What do you mean?"

"We must drive them from the dig."

"How do you propose that we accomplish that?"

The next morning they armed twenty-three of their Negroes. After Jeff had trained them in the art of firearms and combat for three days, he led them in an attack. The matter was not the pitched battle they feared, because upon seeing Jeff leading a charge with armed slaves supporting him, the men fled and never returned. Years later when Jeff was president of the Confederacy, he proposed during the early days of the war that the

South arm the slaves to fight for Southern independence in return for granting them their freedom. The Confederate Congress turned a deaf ear to this proposal until the lasts months of the conflict when it was too late to turn the tide of the war.

In the fall of 1837, after two years of burying himself in farming, Jeff's grief receded. He realized that he missed the comrades he had enjoyed in the army. At this time, he received correspondence from a former comrade-in-arms. There stood a possibility that congress would authorize two new infantry regiments to address a boundary dispute with Great Britain and to deal with the increasing attacks from Indians in the Southwest. Jeff realized this might be an opportunity to see military action again.

Jeff waited for the right opportunity to discuss the subject with Joseph. He found the courage to do so during the first week in November when they were sitting in the library beside the fireplace which emitted enough heat to keep even this large room warm during this unusually cold day.

"I plan to leave next week on an extended trip."

Joseph was taken by surprised by this announcement.

"Where are you going?"

"To New York, Philadelphia, Baltimore, and then on to Washington."

Joseph knew when he mentioned Washington that Jeff had more in mind than just a vacation tour.

"What's this trip really about?

When Jeff divulged why he planned to visit the capital, Joseph was stunned. He now realized that his brother had not yet settled on his life's course, and he was glad he still retained the title to *Brierfield*.

"You must seek your own destiny," he said and then changed the subject to other matters.

* * *

Jeff became sick during his journey. By the time he reached Washington on December 23, he was so ill that he took to his bed. He did not venture out until New Year's Day when he went to an open house at the executive mansion. It was so crowded that he left early without even speaking to President Van Buren. Two days later, feeling better, he went to Dowson's boarding house on Capitol Hill, where his old friend from Transylvania University, George Jones, now a Congressman from Iowa, shared rooms with Thomas Hart Benton. Jones persuaded Jeff to board with him during his stay in Washington. Using the boarding house as his base of operations, Jeff contacted individuals who could use their influence to help him get a commission when the new regiments were formed.

While Jeff waited for some news on his request, he made the acquaintance of a congressman from New Hampshire named Franklin Pierce. They became close friends. Franklin frequently accompanied Jeff and Jones as they made the social rounds attending the various parties held in the capital every evening. This pleasant time was marred by only one distasteful event. In late February, Jones took Jeff to watch a duel between Representative Cilley of Maine, a close friend of Pierce, and William Graves of Kentucky. He watched as Cilley, who was inexperienced with a firearm, was killed by Graves, a known marksman. This death did not change Jeff's view that dueling should be allowed as a last option when necessary to defend one's honor.

In March, Jeff who had suffered from insomnia since Knoxie's death, stayed late at a reception given by Secretary of War Joel Poinsett. Senator Allen from Ohio and he remained for a late supper with their host after the other guests had departed. When the evening grew very late, Jeff began to feel ill. He left in the company of Allen. In the darkness, Allen stepped off the side of a bridge and fell into the shallow Tiber Creek, landing on his feet. Jeff also fell, but landed on his head. Allen emerged unhurt, but Jeff suffered cuts and bruises. Once they were back at the boarding house a doctor was summoned. By the time he arrived, Jeff had a swelling where his head had hit the bottom. The doctor diagnosed him as having a concussion. Before the doctor could leave, Jeff fell into a state of unconsciousness which lasted for several hours. On the advice of the doctor, he remained in bed for three days. When he was back on his feet, Pierce arranged for him to have breakfast with President Van Buren. Jeff pressed his request for a commission if new infantry regiments were created, but the president never committed to help him.

It was early April when Jeff received word that only one regiment would be authorized, and that all officers' slots had been filled by those on active duty. Disappointed, he went to Pittsburg where he boarded a boat for the long trip back to Davis Bend. While he had not achieved his objective, he had renewed his ties to past acquaintances and socialized with the great men of his day. The seed of a desire to participate in the political life of his country had been planted, and it would grow until it consumed him.

* * *

When he returned to Mississippi, Jeff found Joseph was depressed and melancholy. He was in an unsettled state about his wife, Eliza. The age difference between them was causing difficulty as the couple made the transition between Joseph treating her as a child, to allowing her the space to be a wife with her own opinions and goals. The marital strife was so unsettling to Jeff that he moved into the cottage he had started to build for Knoxie and began its completion.

Jeff began to assume a normal life upon his return. He worked hard to make his land productive and began to interact with society around him by attending social events on neighboring plantations. The word quickly spread, and soon parents made sure their available daughters were attending for Jefferson Davis was considered the most eligible man in the area. At one of these events, he was introduced to Varina Howell for the first time. He had already admired her beauty from a distance that evening. She stood out, because like her brothers, she was very tall. When their eyes met, he immediately knew he would have more than a passing interest in her. Unfortunately, for the rest of the night he had no opportunity to engage her in discussion, because Jeff was widely known to be the best ballroom dancer, and he was in great demand. Varina watched his dancing skills with admiration, but she was frequently interrupted by men who had dance cards with her name upon them. By the end of the evening the curiosity of both had been aroused, and soon there would be an opportunity for them to meet again.

On occasion when the work on his plantation allowed him, Jeff visited Louisville and Hot Springs. Soon politics interrupted his traveling out of state and his focus on the plantation. The campaign of 1840 pitted the Democrat, President Van Buren against the Whig, William Henry Harrison. Jeff witnessed some of the campaign speeches in person, since a leader of the Whigs, Henry Clay, made several visits to the Natchez and Vicksburg area. Jeff, although a Democrat, wasn't fond of Van Buren. Though it was not a burning issue, the issues of slavery raised its head in a national election, and for the first time the proponents of States' Rights were tarred with its defense. After the War Between the States, historians viewing the discord would fail to distinguish between the concept of a defense of states' sovereignty and the defense of slavery.

The two years after the election were peaceful ones for Jeff. His plantation was prospering, with James acting as the overseer. It had been seven years since he had lost Knoxie, and he had recovered enough to look forward, instead of wresting with the demons that had haunted him after her death. He traveled during the sick season to Lexington, Kentucky and to places as far away as Wisconsin. He also spent time in the Northeast. Finally at the age of thirty-five, he dove into politics. He became active in the democratic circles in his area, and when the Democratic candidate for the legislature withdrew at the last minute, Jeff was drafted to fill the spot on the ticket. Even though the district was a Whig stronghold, with only a few weeks left in the campaign, he was still able to capture 512 votes out of 1, 197 casts. This was a respectable 43% of the ballots. This defeat was not seen as a setback by either Jeff or his friends. It was apparent to all with knowledge of politics in the state that Jeff had a bright political future ahead of him.

* * *

Joseph decided after Jeff returned from Washington that his brother needed an anchor to keep him from straying too far from *Brierfield*. What better anchor was there than a wife who was from the area. In December 1843, when Jeff decided to attend the party caucus in Vicksburg, he received a note from Joseph to meet him at Diamond Place, a plantation owned by Joseph's daughter, Florida. They would travel to the convention together from there. Jeff was unaware that Joseph had set in motion a plan involving Varina Howell, the seventeen year-old he had briefly met at a party.

Varina was the daughter of Joseph's longtime friend William Howell. The Howell family had prospered in Mississippi and had a home named Briers on the bluff at Natchez. Varina's family had strong political connections. Her grandfather had once been the governor of New Jersey. The Howells had a high opinion of Jeff having met him when they accompanied Joseph to West Point on a visit. The night of the party they had noticed with pleasure the look in Jeff's eyes when their daughter was introduced to him.

Jeff was immediately taken with this attractive young woman during his stay at Diamond Point. He overlooked the fact that Varina was half his age. Instead, he focused on her olive skin complexion, handsome figure, full lips, and sultry looks and the way she carried herself with confidence. He attributed these physical traits to the fact that one of Varina's ancestors was from the southwest region of Wales. He had often heard that many Welsh beauties came from that gene pool to which the Basque and Celtics had contributed. Her physical attributes could not have been more different than Knoxie's. However, Varina's strong will and her independent nature did remind him of Knoxie. Perhaps this particular similarity was because both women had received an education from elite schools, something that most American women did not have the privilege of having access to.

After Jeff and Joseph departed for Vicksburg, Varina wrote a letter to her mother.

Dear Mama,

I arrived safely. A few hours later Joseph's brother, Jefferson Davis, who I understand you are favorably acquainted with, came riding in on a beautiful white horse. He was meeting Joseph here, and the two are going to a Vicksburg political meeting, where delegates will be selected for the State Democratic Convention He was so fashionably dressed that I can see why my friends are all trying to attract his attention. I'm not sure whether I like him. He does not have the charm of his brother, Joseph. His demeanor at times makes him appear older than he could possibly be. Yet there were times that I did enjoy his company during the two days he was here before they left for Vicksburg. He seems always guarded in his conduct, but I believe he is a person of good character. I do not think I shall ever like him as much as his brother.

Florida was so kind to invite me to spend another week, so I will not be coming home Sunday.

Love,
Varina

* * *

Jeff was in love. When the busy activities of the caucus were over, he returned to his plantation, but his thoughts were constantly on Varina. It clouded his mind to the point that it interfered with his daily routine. Finally he asked Joseph to invite her to come and visit *Hurricane* for a few days. Joseph was happy to see his matchmaking had produced a positive result. It never occurred to him that the problems in his own marriage caused by the great difference in age might present Jeff with the same issue if he married Varina. Strangely, it also never deterred Jeff, for he was lonely and his heart ached to see her again.

Varina arrived in the latter part of January and stayed for three weeks. Only when she received a letter from her parents demanding that she return home, did she have Joseph make arrangements for her to depart on a steamboat that was stopping at Davis Bend. She had enjoyed her visit. During the evenings, Varina had sat with Jeff and Joseph in the library and listened while Jeff read aloud to his brother from copies of Congressional debates. Sometimes, she read materials to the two men. Unlike many women of her culture, she was an educated person who was alert to the interests of the day, and her sharp intellect added meat to the conversation. She even enjoyed their other discussions that covered such diverse topics as agriculture and the law.

The weeks had passed too fast for Jeff. He could hardly bear to see her go. He had enjoyed the daily horseback rides and the strolls through the fruit orchards that lay near the home. Previously, he had avoided the idea of another mate since Knoxie's death. Now he realized how foolish that had been.

When Varina told him that she must return to Natchez, he got on his knees and proposed. While she did not give him an outright yes, she did indicate that her feelings lay in that direction. He wanted to come to Briers to propose formally to her after securing her parents' permission. She felt that would not be a good idea.

"Just wait until I have had an opportunity to speak with them. I'll write and let you know when to come."

The day the steamboat docked, Jeff waited with other members of his family and watched her board. Even at this late moment, he hoped for a hand signal that would invite him aboard to go to Brier with her, but she gave no indication she desired him there. His heart sank.

Varina had mixed emotions as the boat reached the middle of the Mississippi. She liked Jeff, but she wasn't sure that she should accept his proposal. The difference in their ages was only one factor. During her stay, she had seen how Joseph treated his wife, Eliza, like a child, instructing, judging, reproving, and speaking to her like a father. From that point on, Varina's affection for Joseph began to diminish. She was offended when she thought Jeff exhibited this same attitude toward her on occasion during her stay. She was strong-willed, and even her parents did not dictate to her.

Back in Natchez, Varina wrestled with her emotions. In the short time they had been apart, she had missed him. She delayed replying to his correspondence until she could decide her feelings on the issue of marriage. If she made a decision to accept Jeff's proposal, she would then have to convince her parents. She knew that her father would not be an obstacle. Her mother was a different story. After all, Jeff was only two years younger than her mother.

Margret Howell understood the problems of a marriage where there was such a great age difference. While she liked Joseph, she would never have put up with being treated like Eliza, and she was afraid Jeff might have the same traits. There was another issue. Her own husband was much older. In the past they had a good marriage, but the intimacy was no longer there. It was a physical thing. If her daughter married Jeff, she could expect he would also suffer the same physical impairment in his fifties. She wondered if Joseph had developed any problems in that regard. She doubted it. He always showed such great vigor. She regretted not pursuing him with more determination.

Life did not return to normal for Jeff after Varina's departure. He was bored and became melancholy. He wrote her several letters, but she did not reply. When he was about to give up hope, a steamboat docked at Davis Bend during March and delivered a letter from Varina. This immediately dispelled his gloominess, even though she told him not to come to Briers just yet. He wrote back, "I am willing on this matter to be guided by you."

The courtship continued through correspondences. Jeff treasured her letters that often contained a lock of her hair or flowers she had pressed between the pages. By the end of March, she not only consented to his proposal but had also persuaded her mother, thus leaving Jeff free to come to Natchez at last.

In April, Jeff arrived at the Howell residence and formally received Varina's and her parents' consent. The next week the engagement was announced in the Natchez newspaper. The date for the wedding was set for the next year in the spring of 1844. The wait was not Jeff's idea, for he did not want to delay, but the Howells and Varina were adamant. It turned out to be a good thing because for the next several months Jeff would be involved in the grip of politics.

* * *

In January 1844 Jeff had attended the State Democratic Convention as a delegate. Despite the fact that the county slate was pledged to Van Buren, he broke rank and made a speech supporting John C. Calhoun of South Carolina. This was the first time that Jeff revealed in public his strongly held beliefs that the executive branch in Washington had become too powerful and constituted a growing threat to state sovereignty. This worry was being compounded because Southern control of the national government had ended. The South's representation in Congress had been permanently reduced to minority status. Jeff declared in a speech to the convention, "We are daily becoming weaker, and the concept of federalism is being battered down by those who believe political power should reside in Washington and not the states." His now declared public views placed him on the side of the strict constructionists, who opposed any federal interference in state matters, not specifically granted in the Constitution. His actions also revealed his philosophy concerning the duty of a representative. Despite the fact that he had been elected by the county Democrats to support Van Buren, he supported the man he believed was the best candidate. The rest of his public life, his actions were always based on what he believed to be the proper course and not the will of his constituents.

The day after the convention, Jeff made a public address arguing in favor of the annexation of Texas. Later, when Polk was selected to be the presidential candidate, Jeff set off on a grueling season of stump meetings. He spoke at public rallies in favor of the Democratic ticket of Polk, the party's platform of annexing Texas, opposition to a national bank, and for the reform of laws that were oppressive to the southern states. He worked himself to exhaustion and suffered a recurrence of malaria. After a few weeks of respite, Jeff continued to campaign throughout the state. Whenever he spoke in the vicinity of Natchez, Varina was always present.

The speaking gained him statewide recognition, and he developed a popular following among those who feared federal encroachment. Although he was never seen as a friend of the common man because his time spent in schools away from the activities of everyday life had made him part of an elite, most who heard him speak were impressed with his sincerity.

During the campaign, Jeff had only three private visits with Varina, although he had been seen with her publicly at several political gatherings. Varina did not mince words about Jeff's obsession with politics whenever they were alone. She did not like the fact that it had proven to be a distraction from his attention to her. They also had long discussions about where they would live. She did not want to live even temporarily at *Hurricane*, nor the simple cottage at *Brierfield* that Jeff had described to her. She was used to the more sophisticated life in Natchez, and wasn't interested in being isolated in the rural confines near Davis Bend. Jeff had no choice. A planter, who was still developing his plantation, had to be on site. So despite her reservations, plans were made to live at *Brierfield*, and Jeff promised to commence work immediately on a suitable home for them.

* * *

Varina had developed an intense dislike for Joseph, a man whom she had once thought to be so charming. She was jealous of the close relationship between Jeff and Joseph, and she did not like the way he treated his wife. When her father had a falling out with Joseph over a business transaction, she wanted nothing more to do with her husband's brother. Despite the rupture of this relationship, she decided to go through with her commitment to marry Jeff. Both became impatient and decided not to wait until spring.

In February, Jeff boarded a steamboat for Natchez where he was to be married. Much to his surprise, one of the passengers was Zachary Taylor. When Taylor saw Jeff come aboard, he approached him and extended his hand. In that moment the two reconciled. Taylor had just visited Knoxie's grave, and now he was on his way to the border between Texas and Mexico.

When Jeff arrived in Natchez he found Varina ill. The marriage would have to be delayed. Two days later, he returned home.

My Daring Jeff,

I felt dreadfully sorry that our wedding had to be postponed. My illness was of a most embarrassing kind. It has taken weeks for my health to recover. But now that I am well, I wait impatiently for you, my darling. As soon as you can, please book passage on a steamer heading in this direction. I shall be waiting to become your loving wife.

Keeping you in my thoughts every moment of each day, as I wait for your return.

Love,
Varina

At ten in the morning on February 26, Jeff and Varina stood before her family at Briers. Varina wore an engagement ring that Jeff had purchased during a trip to New Orleans, and jewels she had inherited from her grandmother. The minister from the local Episcopal Church performed the wedding. After the ceremony, the family sat down to a breakfast before they boarded a steamer for Locust Grove.

Anna was surprised when they appeared at her door that evening. She had never met Varina, but she was aware of the Howell family and had received word from Eliza of the engagement.

"Come in my dear," she said. "What an unexpected pleasure to meet you at last. I feel like we are already friends from the correspondences I've received from Jeff's family over the past few weeks."

Varina was relieved by the open friendliness of Anna's reception. She had dreaded spending the first day of their marriage in the home where Knoxie had died. When Jeff had disclosed his plans in one of his letters, she could not find the words to express her objections. She also felt it was kind of morbid that he felt a duty to visit his first wife's grave with her. But her mother had warned that she must not pit herself in a power contest with the memory of a dead woman, because she would only damage the feelings Jeff had toward her.

Anna found Varina charming but quite different from what she had experienced when she met Knoxie at *Hurricane*. Then Jeff's young bride had hung onto his every word, and her eyes had a certain glow about them whenever Jeff acknowledged her presence. She did not notice these things about Varina, though the young bride was very pleasant and did show Jeff the type of respect that a married woman should in the presence of others.

The next morning Jeff took Varina to Knoxie's grave. They stood before it for a long time. Jeff remained silent and bowed his head. Then he turned and faced her. She could see the remnants of dried tears upon his face.

"I will always love her."

"I know," she said.

Strangely, she admired the love he still felt for Knoxie. Varina knew she could never fill the space Knoxie had in her husband's heart, but she realized there was enough room in his heart for both of them. They left the grave with their arms around each other, and he never mentioned his first wife to her again.

After two days at Locust Grove, the newlyweds went to Woodville where they visited Jeff's mother at Rosemont. Jane was now in her eighties and quite frail. It was apparent she would not be long for this world. They spent several days with Jane and paid her a great deal of attention. Varina saw another soft side of Jeff. She realized that just below his exterior, he was a complex man and only in time would she be able to understand all the elements of his personality.

The morning the couple was leaving, Jane informed them that she had two years earlier been confirmed in the Episcopal Church by Jeff's old friend from West Point, Leonidas Polk. This came as a surprise to Jeff, for his mother had always been a staunch Baptist, but he also remembered the persuasive power of Leonidas. After the couple left Rosemont, they began their honeymoon by boarding a steamer for New Orleans where they planned to spend a month.

"It's beautiful," Varina exclaimed when the coachman stopped in front of the hotel. It was grand, for Jeff had spared no expense when he had secured accommodations weeks in advance of his wedding. As they waited for their trunks to be brought into the reception area, each was impressed by the decor and the sight of so many well-dressed people constantly entering and exiting the premises. After Jeff was given the keys, and their luggage was delivered to the room, Jeff escorted Varina to a restaurant on Charles Street for their evening meal. The waiter delivered to their table a vast array of different cuisine, but each ate so sparingly that the server asked them if there was something wrong with the food. It wasn't the food. Jeff always ate very little, and Varina was nervous about spending their first night together. They had been forced by circumstances to sleep in separate bedrooms since their wedding. The couple had an understanding that they would not consummate their marriage until their honeymoon.

Jeff had champagne sent up to the room, and they sat out on the balcony that overlooked a busy street below. They were on the fifth floor which placed them high enough that the unpleasant odors of the streets did not reach them and spoil the atmosphere. The moon was full and the sound of music from a nearby establishment reached their ears. It was a romantic evening, and Jeff did not let any serious conversation spoil the moment. Instead, he read to his wife two poems he had composed for her. She was surprised by his ability and touched by the words. When the moment was right, he excused himself and went downstairs to give her some privacy while she prepared herself for the marital bed.

Alone in the room, Varina removed from her trunk the beautiful nightgown her mother had purchased. The material was silk, and it had been made in Paris. There was a matching undergarment. After bathing herself with water in the wash basin, she put on perfume, which was also from Paris. She liked the smell, and it made her feel a little adventurous. She hoped it would have the same effect on Jeff. She wasn't afraid of what women always said was the pain when one lost their virginity. Her mother had given her a book to read on matters involving how to please your husband in bed. She was confident from what she had read that she would be able to please him. She blew out all the candles, except one that she placed in a position to accent the beauty of her breasts. Her gown was designed to give them substantial exposure. Then she sat up in the bed and waited for her husband to return.

Jeff finished the bath he had arranged downstairs and asked the barber to give him a clean shave and to place cologne upon his face. Prepared as best he could, he returned to the room.

The first thing Jeff noticed was Varina's lack of nervousness as she removed her gown. When they made love, the spontaneity of his first night with Knoxie was missing. But Varina's body was much more developed, and she seemed determined to please him. They made love a second time that same night. Something he had never experienced with a woman before.

Varina lay beside her husband in the quietness of the night. The lone candle that she had left burning was now extinguished. She knew she had pleased him, but what surprised her more was that he had given her pleasure to a degree she never imagined possible. She lay there in the dark for some time reliving the passion she had felt, then she dozed off to sleep.

The honeymoon came to an end, and the couple boarded a steam boat for Davis Bend to begin their life in the cottage that Jeff had originally designed for Knoxie at *Brierfield*. When the steamer docked, the Davis clan, having had advance notice of their expected arrival, was waiting beneath the trees near the wharf. They rode in style in a coach that had been decorated with flowers harvested from the garden at *Hurricane*. When they reached Joseph's home, many slaves from *Brierfield* were there, for they were anxious to see what their new mistress looked like. They gathered around the coach and cheered her as she stepped onto the gravel driveway. She walked onto the porch and waved to them. Much to the surprise of Jeff and Joseph, she delivered a short speech, thanking everyone for showing her such a welcome.

The morning after their arrival, Jeff and Varina rode their horses on the old Indian trail that connected *Hurricane* with their plantation. As they emerged from the woods, Varina saw for the first time the structure that would be their home. It stood in the middle of a grove of large oaks. Jeff had designed it in a manner that tested his thoughts on architecture. He structured it to be efficient for the climate. It was built in the style of the old Spanish colonial homes but with such innovative features as outer doorways six feet wide to allow the flow of as much cool air as possible. Inside the rooms were large, and each contained enormous fireplaces. Although Jeff had promised to commence work immediately on a proper plantation home, they would spend three years in this structure before the other was completed.

THE CONGRESSMAN

In July the time arrived for the County Democratic Convention. Joseph and Jeff attended and were selected as delegates to the State Convention. Varina was not happy that Jeff would now be going to Jackson for another political function. Despite her tears and when that didn't work, her temper, he went anyway. He was beginning to realize that his wife's immaturity coupled with an independent streak did not bode well for domestic tranquility.

When the State Democratic Convention met in Jackson, Jeff already knew that his friends had secretly conspired to put his name forward as a candidate for Congress. Jeff had become well known to the political operatives in the state, and with the weight of Joseph's connections, defeated the other candidates.

Jeff was on the campaign trail again. At this time in history, Mississippi congressional candidates were elected statewide. The next several months found Jeff attending daylong barbecues and stump meetings in every part of the state. His platform was centered on issues that were dear to his heart. He opposed high tariffs, which enriched Northern industry at the cost of the South. He advocated that tariffs only be collected which were necessary for the operation of the federal government. He also opposed laws that took funds from the sale of government lands and scattered the proceeds among the states, because he believed that it would create a dependency on Washington and subvert state sovereignty. His platform embraced the concept of manifest destiny believing it was God's intent that the United States boundaries should reach from the Atlantic to the Pacific.

* * *

In the short five months of their marriage, Varina had been deprived of Jeff's company most of the time. A bride who was barely nineteen, she did not have the maturity to understand his actions. She wanted attention, and she was not getting it from a man who was old enough to be her father. She wrote many letters complaining to her friends in Natchez.

"I know the bitterness of being a politician's wife. Jeff's desire to go to Washington has darkened the sunlight that I so expected the first year of our marriage and has left me alone isolated at *Brierfield*."

It would take some time before she accepted the intensity and passion that seized Jeff when he committed himself to something. Varina did not get to see him except for two weeks when he came home sick from a recurring bout of malaria and an inflamed left eye. She nursed him back to health, and in September he left to campaign again. Her husband had a passion for public service, and despite the absence from Varina, illness from exposure, and opponents' defamation on his character, he would always remain a public figure.

At last the campaign was over. It had exacted a heavy toll on Jeff's health, but the effort had been worth it. Jeff had been elected to congress, and already people were calling him the Calhoun of Mississippi. Something in Jeff had touched the voters, and he would in time become in their minds and in the minds of other Southerners, the personification of their ideas and beliefs. Even before Calhoun died, they would see him as the replacement of the old sage from South Carolina.

Jeff and Varina made plans to leave for Washington. The oath would be taken by the new congress in the capital on November 30th. Jeff, who had planned to arrive two weeks before that date, changed his mind when he learned that John C. Calhoun was expected to deliver a speech in Vicksburg on November 10th. Unfortunately, at the last minute Calhoun's arrival was delayed until November 18. When he finally arrived, the Lion of the Senate was entertained by the Howells. Smitten by Varina, Calhoun rarely left her side. Afterwards, when he returned to Washington, they carried on a relationship by correspondence until his death.

It had been a wise political move to wait in Mississippi until Calhoun's arrival. The Senator would remember him primarily because of the infatuation with his wife, but to the public they would appear to have adopted the role of mentor and pupil.

Once Calhoun departed Vicksburg, Jeff had no time to waste. He boarded a steamship along with Varina and congressman-elect Robert Johnson. The steamer was scheduled to take them to Ohio. From there, the party planned to take passage on a train to Wheeling, Virginia and thence to Washington by coach. But the steamer had problems with a boiler and it took five days just to get to Cairo, Illinois, The party changed to another steamer and started up the Ohio. Unfortunately, on the second day of the journey the weather turned cold, and the channel was blocked by ice. During the next several days they stayed on board and hoped that the temperature would warm and the ice thaw. When this did not happen, they transferred to a smaller boat. After steaming all night, it had progressed only a few hundred yards. Realizing the only way to continue was by land, they left the ship and purchased a large wooden sled. Placing their trunks upon it, the three sat on them, while two horses pulled the sled over the rough road toward Wheeling. A few miles later, as the horses were pulling the sled up a high bank, it overturned, sending the three down the steep slope.

Jeff found himself buried in a snow bank. When he struggled out of it, he saw his wife lying motionless a few yards away. Fear struck his heart. "Varina!" he cried out, as he ran toward her.

Recovering from being knocked out when her head hit a rock, Varina was brought back to reality by Jeff's voice in the distance.

"Jeff, help me."

"My love," he said, as he took her in his arms.

Her face was badly bruised, and there was a swelling on her forehead.

"Where's Robert?" she asked.

In Jeff's concern about his wife, he had completely forgotten about their friend. He lay not too far away, and was still recovering from the shock of impact.

"I think a rib's broken," Jeff said, as his fingers pressed against a right rib.

"We must get something out of the sled and wrap him tight." he told Varina.

Once again the sled was moving forward. Varina and Robert rode while Jeff followed. Many times during the rest of the trip he had to push the sled through the layers of mud created by the melting snow. When their food supplies became exhausted, Jeff had to scrounge the area to buy food. Nothing was available but milk, sausage, and maple syrup, and the three sustained themselves on this. When they reached Wheeling, Jeff hired a coach, and they finally arrived in Washington after more than three weeks of traveling.

Jeff made arrangements for temporary quarters at the National Hotel, until he could find more suitable quarters. The next day on December 8, he appeared at the congressional building with Robert. They were given the oath of office by the Clerk of the House. As a new member of

Congress, Jeff was assigned to the very back row beside Robert. His seat was a small mahogany desk and arm chair. Around the room were twenty-two columns of beautiful marble, and above was a magnificent dome. At the front of the room was the elevated desk of the speaker with the portraits of Washington and Lafayette placed on the wall behind it. Seated in front of Jeff was Armistead L. Burt, a new congressman from Abbeville, South Carolina. They became friends the first day of the session.

One late evening when Jeff and Armistead were having drinks at the hotel, a tall, gaunt gentleman came by on his way to the staircase that led to the rooms above.

"Do you know who that is?" asked Armistead, who was highly intoxicated.

"Abraham Lincoln. He's the Whig Congressman from Illinois," Jeff said.

"Not only that but he is John C. Calhoun's son."

"You're drunk Armistead. You had better watch your words. What you said is a dueling offense."

"But it's true. Common knowledge back home. His mother Nancy Hanks was from my home area near Abbeville. She was the daughter of Luke and Ann Hanks. Calhoun was a young lawyer and traveled around a lot to the various courthouses. He used to stop for the night at Orr's tavern for good food, liquor, and a room for the night. Nancy worked there, and the two struck up a relationship. When she turned up pregnant, her family wanted to put her out of the house, but she begged them to send her to live with her aunt in Kentucky. Lucky for Calhoun that about that time a man named Tom Lincoln from Kentucky showed up with some Tennessee hogs for sale. Calhoun paid him a sum of money to take Nancy, her daughter, and the unborn child to the aunt's place in Kentucky. Before she left, Nancy had Calhoun sign an agreement to pay support for the child when it was born. She recorded the agreement in the courthouse before she left the county. Later Nancy wrote her parents that Tom and she had married."

"I hope you won't remember this story tomorrow," Jeff said.

"Calhoun and Lincoln even look alike, and both suffer from Marfan syndrome," Armistead said.

* * *

Even at the beginning of his service in Congress, Jeff was noticed. His tall slender body carried a soldierly bearing that attracted immediate attention. His intellectual grasp of national affairs won him the respect of the other members. In the social setting, his cultural refinement made him a welcome guest at the few events he attended, fewer than Varina would have liked. Instead, Jeff spent many hours at his desk answering correspondences from his constituents. When he arrived home, he generally buried himself in material that would increase his knowledge of issues before the congress. He liked to micro-manage everything, and he could not seem to distinguish between matters that were great or small. Later this trait would play an important role in Jeff's public and private life.

Unlike other freshmen congressmen, Jeff did not hesitate to rise and speak from the floor of the House. He already possessed in abundance a well-thought-out philosophy on issues facing the nation. When the Know-Nothing party introduced a bill to restrict the rights of immigrants to full citizenship, he immediately rose to his feet to object.

"I am opposed to a law that would delay citizenship, from the current five years, to twenty-one years. The proposal that only persons born in this country can hold public office, I find repugnant. The immigration laws should be modified, but only to make the process of naturalization more easily accomplished. If we admit foreigners, but deny them the enjoyment of all political rights, we stand the possibility of creating a large pool of persons who will become enemies of our government, and this country will soon become filled with discontented men."

Jeff had been in Washington only a month when Varina and he were invited to a private dinner with President Polk and his wife Sarah at the executive mansion. This was a favorite method of Polk. He had private dinners frequently with the powerful members of Congress, but he also reached out to any new members that he believed would quickly gather a following about them.

"How do I look?" a nervous Varina asked.

"Like the prettiest woman in Washington."

A private coach delivered them to the front steps of the executive mansion. A doorman escorted Jeff and Varina to the parlor. Shortly thereafter, the president and his wife appeared.

No one could have been better suited for the role of First Lady than Sarah Polk. She spoke to them as if they were the best of friends. While the men talked she gave Varina a tour of the home.

"Everything is so lovely," Varina said.

"It's a big improvement from the way it was when we arrived. The Congress provided funds, and now this house is something we can present to the world without shame."

"I'm so thankful for the president's invitation."

"Well it's not all social. James knows a rising star when he sees one. Varina, your husband will go far in public life."

Sarah knew with that one comment, she had made an ally of the congressman's wife.

That night, as Varina lay in bed beside Jeff, she was filled with excitement. She always admired Jeff, but now she knew even the powerful of Washington recognized his abilities.

Perhaps I should not be so hard on him for not spending time with me, she thought. After all, he may be president one day.

* * *

Though it was unusual for a new member to take an active role in his first term, Jeff did not feel bound by such mores. In February, he addressed his colleagues when he distanced himself from the war hawks.

"I believe in manifest destiny, but the country should not rush into war with Great Britain. Nor should these United States engage in aggressive acts toward Mexico. War should be the last resort of any nation."

While this seemed a departure from the rhetoric of his campaign, Jeff always felt a man should vote his conscience after he had thoroughly examined all sides of an issues. His constituents had elected him to use his own good judgment, even though his assessment might not reflect their views. After his speech, men from both parties clustered around his desk and shook his hand. The applause he received showed the political world that in the future this would be a man to be reckoned with.

Jeff made friends with men of all political persuasions. Even if they didn't agree with him, they appreciated his depth of knowledge on subjects that were important to them and the logic in his positions. He quickly made friends with a Whig representative, John Quincy Adams, who had served in the House since he failed to win re-election to the presidency. They became particularly close while serving together on a committee that studied the issue of whether to accept a five million dollar bequest from James Smithson to these United States to use in establishing a Smithsonian Institution; an organization whose purpose would be to increase knowledge among men. The fund had been held in limbo for many years because the government had failed to make a decision on whether to accept it. Although Jeff firmly believed most education was a matter of state concern, and he opposed any federal control of it, he did not see how anyone could be against a national institute that would spread knowledge to the American people. He saw this as an opportunity to draw the people of the republic closer together. It was a struggle to get the bill approving the institution through the House. Even though he was only a freshman, he became the point man for the legislation, and it was because of his determination that the Smithsonian was finally established. Jeff would continue throughout his political life in Washington to be an ardent supporter.

Although Jeff had been cast as the Calhoun of Mississippi, he broke with the senator over the issue of federal expenditures for harbors and rivers. Once again he was at odds with his constituents who would bene-fit from such action, but he voted as his view of the constitution required.

"The federal government is a creature of the states and has no inher-ent powers," he said in a speech before the House. "The only power it holds is that given by the states. The constitution is not one of limitations on the national government, but it is a document of grants of power to that government. The states can grant or withhold power from it or even dissolve it."

While Jeff held such views, this did not deter him from always being a strong proponent of the United States military. At every opportunity he strove to increase its strength. His bill to create rifle regiments was defeated leaving soldiers with the outdated muskets that had been used in the War of 1812. This only stiffened Jeff's reluctance to be a war hawk since he believed that the American military was unprepared to fight the British over Oregon territory or face Santa Anna's large Mexican Army. Despite being a States' Righter, he did not have the same faith in the state militia held by his fellow Southerners. He was a West Point man, and therefore always held a bias against those who had never been trained as professional soldiers.

* * *

Varina enjoyed Washington. It was a different world from the one she had faced alone and isolated at *Brierfield*. She would have liked to have partici-pated more in the social life of the capital. Instead she had to spend many evening at home because Jeff had buried himself in his work, and she was much younger than the other wives so they rarely included her in their activities. She spent her days shopping and visiting the museum and other points of interest. Sometimes she would attend sessions of the House. She even saw Jeff make a couple of speeches, until he told her how nervous she made him watching from the gallery. The only time they spent a lot of time together was when he was sick. That happened several times when Jeff had a recurrence of malaria. She would spend days nursing him back to health. He especially suffered during these times from terrific pain in his left eye. He was already beginning to permanently lose sight in it.

* * *

In early May news reached Washington that United States troops had been attacked on American soil. The unit involved was Jeff's old regiment. Two companies had been either killed or captured. Congress was furious, and patriotic emotion swept the Capitol. The next day President Polk announced to Congress that a state of war existed with Mexico. Now Jeff supported the war wholeheartedly believing American honor was at stake, and that Mexico was intent on conquering Texas. The president was authorized by Congress to vigorously prosecute the war, which he did by immediately calling upon the states to organize militias and send them to assist the army. He requested twenty thousand volunteers from the Deep South and the states along the Mississippi. Another thirty thousand men were requested from the rest of the nation. During the furor of the next few days, a recent bill Jeff had introduced to create two rifle regiments was reported out of committee and passed both Houses of Congress.

Jeff had been restless ever since word of the attack reached Washington. He confided to his friends that he wanted to return to Mississippi and join a regiment that was being raised for the war, but he knew Varina's feelings on this matter, and she would not be easily swayed to change her opinion.

Varina wrote her friends back in Natchez.

"I know how Jeff will react to the news of this conflict. I will use ever method at my disposal to try and discourage him from leaving the Congress."

They had not spent a long time together in their short marriage, and Varina could not bear the thought of being separated from him again. There was also the question of his health. She was afraid he would become ill and perhaps die in a foreign land. In war, one never knew who would be injured, killed, or die from sickness.

For many days the atmosphere between them was so tense that Jeff and Varina did not speak. When the couple received copies of the *Vicksburg Sentinel* calling upon her state's favorite son to come home and lead the regiment, Varina knew the die was cast. Still emotional about losing him, she could not accept it. In a last effort after a heated argument over the matter, Varina left Jeff and went to visit friends who were vacationing in New Hampshire. She remained there for several weeks. Finally realizing this separation would not change Jeff's mind, she returned to Washington.

While Varina was in New Hampshire, Jeff was appointed to serve on a joint congressional committee investigating financial misdeeds. Many who had not yet ascertained the character of Jeff were surprised when he argued against a reprimand and voted in favor of Daniel Webster, even though the man was a Whig and an enemy of the South. In a speech from the floor he said, "I could not vote otherwise than as I perceived the evidence."

The men who volunteered in the states and territories were so numerous that President Polk had to limit the number of regiments that would be accepted in federal service. Although Mississippi was limited to one regiment, the response to a call for 1,000 volunteers was so great that by June 1, over 17,000 men were in Vicksburg to enlist. When the governor's request to allow his state to create five additional regiments was denied, he asked to fill the quota given other states that had not been filled. This also met with no success. So a lottery was held and resulted in a regiment of ten companies composed of one hundred men each.

Some congressmen who favored the militia over the regular army made negative comments about the officer corps, which was comprised of many West Point graduates. When one such comment was made in a speech from the floor of Congress, Jeff rose and made a stinging reply.

"Every occupation requires study. West Point trains officers. You should not expect someone without military training like a blacksmith or tailor to be qualified to lead men in battle."

Andrew Johnson, a congressman from Tennessee who had been a tailor, was incensed. He took the floor in the defense of his own profession. The congressman's speech that day did not end the matter. At every opportunity thereafter he attacked Jeff, and for the rest of his life, he hated Jefferson Davis. Jeff could not know how this speech would have an impact upon him later in life.

* * *

In April during a hot debate in the House, Jeff looked up and spotted an old friend from Vicksburg in the gallery. When the representatives took a break, Jeff met him in the hallway. He was handed an envelope. Inside was a message from the governor. The men of the 1st Regiment of Volunteers of Mississippi had elected him their colonel. Enclosed was a list of the companies and the officers.

Company - A - Yazoo Guards
Company - B - Wilkinson Guards
Company - C - Vicksburg Southrons
Company - D - Carroll County Guards
Company - E - Jackson Fencibles
Company - F - Lafayette Guards
Company - G - Raymond Fencibles
Company - H - Vicksburg Volunteers
Company - I - Holly Springs Guards
Company - K -Tombigbee Guards

The list of men included many that Jeff knew from his county, and men he had established contact with during campaigns across the state. The other high ranking officers in the regiment were Lieutenant Colonel McClung and Major Bradford. Jeff had frequent contact with them during political campaigns. The regiment represented the flower of Mississippi. Many members from leading families had accepted the rank of private in their zeal to help their kinsmen in Texas.

The receipt of the correspondence from the governor provided the excuse that Jeff had been waiting for since the news of war reached Washington. He wrote out a reply for his friend to take back to Mississippi. In that letter he accepted the appointment. After the message was safely dispatched, Jeff walked down the street to the executive mansion.

"Mr. President, I plan to leave Washington immediately to join my regiment."

The president encouraged him to stay a few days longer until a proposed tariff act was voted upon. The vote was going to be close, and the president needed Jeff's support. This put Jeff in a position to request equipment for his regiment.

"I'll stay for the vote if you will support my request to arm the First Mississippi with the new modeled rifles produced by the Whitney Arms Company."

"As Commander-in-Chief, I will sign an order to that effect," the president said.

Jeff, from his services on the Arm Services Committee, knew these weapons were more accurate than the old flintlock smoothbores that were standard army issue since the War of 1812. The new rifle used percussion caps and was easier to load. The internal rifling made sure the .54 caliber bullet would travel a long distance with accuracy.

Jeff waited in Washington until the tariff bill finally came up for a vote. The same day of the vote, he received orders from the War Department directing him to take his regiment immediately to Mexico and report to General Zachery Taylor. In the evening, a friend dropped by the boarding house to let him know that another order had been issued to the second-in-command, Lieutenant Colonel Alexander McClung to muster the men and proceed to New Orleans where ships would be waiting to take them to Texas. After his friend left the boarding house, there was a chill in the air, and when Jeff tried to speak to Varina, she burst into tears and fled into the bedroom.

The next morning while Varina was packing, Jeff went to the armory and handed the commanding officer a requisition from him as commander of the First Mississippi Regiment for one thousand of the new rifles, plus other equipment. Attached to it was the directive from the President ordering that the requisition be filled. The next day, July 4th, Jeff and Varina left for Mississippi. They traveled to Pittsburg so he could reach the Mississippi River by way of the Ohio on a steamer. It was not a pleasant trip because the two were in constant strife. Their latest argument centered on where Varina would stay while he was away. Varina wanted to stay with her parents in Natchez, while Jeff insisted she stay at *Hurricane*. Varina did not like her sister-in–law, Eliza, nor Joseph. Finally in frustration, he used a string of profanity so loud that a passenger on the lower deck heard it. Unable to communicate in a civil manner with each other, Jeff buried himself in books on military tactics while Varina stayed in the bedroom and cried constantly.

THE MEXICAN WAR

On July 13th the steamboat reached Vicksburg. Waiting at the dock was James Pemberton with one of the plantation boats that Joseph had sent to bring them to Davis Bend. They spent the night at *Hurricane,* and the next day rode horses to *Brierfield*. James was there waiting to welcome them. He was proud of the progress that had been made in their absence. The cotton seed had been planted and had sprung forth. The garden that Varina had started had been improved and expanded. The slaves gathered in the front yard and were genuinely happy to see Jeff and Varina. He was overwhelmed with emotion when he saw them, and they followed him into the house and gathered around him while he told them of Washington and his plans to go to Mexico and fight in the war.

The slaves already knew about his coming military adventure. Their worry for his safety was tied to their own well-being. He was one of the best masters in Mississippi, and if something happened to him their lives could be changed. Their relationship with Varina was of short duration, and she was young. That meant if she remarried, they would get a new master. The constant fear of being sold was always on their minds. Neither Jeff nor his brother had ever sold a slave. They treated their people like family. Their way of life was dependent upon the slaves, and the welfare of the slaves were dependent upon their master.

After supper that evening, Jeff went down to the first cabin built on the place where he and James had lived together before Jeff married. James was sitting on the front porch of what had now become the Pemberton family home.

"Would you like a cup of coffee?" he asked.

When Jeff indicated yes with a nod of his head, James went into the cabin and returned with two cups. The men sat in rocking chairs and talked about the work done on the plantation, and the project they envisioned for the future.

"James, would you like to go with me to Mexico?"

James had accompanied Jeff in his travels throughout his military career and elsewhere. The only time since West Point that he had not traveled with him was the trip to Washington.

"I think it best that I stay and oversee the plantation and take care of Miss Varina."

Jeff had expected this answer. James was indispensable to *Brierfield*. Several attempts to use a white overseer had failed because of the way they wanted to treat the Negroes. Jeff had fired them. He would not tolerate corporal punishment or any other kind of abuse. His brother had had the same problem. And as a result, Joseph had finally found a slave like James that he could rely on named Ben Montgomery to oversee his plantation. The man was brilliant and self-educated after devouring the written words from the books in Joseph's Library.

Knowing that James would probably want to stay at *Brierfield*, Jeff had mentioned this matter to his brother. Joseph had offered him the service of a slave that he had the greatest confidence in. His name was Jim

Green, and he was married to Montgomery's sister. He showed the same quickness of mind as Montgomery and had become literate through Joseph's efforts. Before he turned in for the night, Jeff sent word to Joseph that he would accept his offer.

Although Jeff would have liked to spend more time at *Brierfield*, he departed the next morning. He had learned when he arrived back in Mississippi that his regiment had already left for New Orleans. He must join them before they reached Mexico. So giving a tearful Varina an embrace and speaking briefly with the Negroes who had gathered in the front yard, James and he departed for *Hurricane* where he would speak a farewell to Joseph and other family members. He would also leave with Joseph a letter addressed to the Speaker of the House resigning his seat in Congress.

"I do not know how long this war will last, Joseph. Just hold it in your possession for a period of time until we see how events develop. I would hate to resign my seat unnecessarily."

In Natchez, Jeff and Jim Green boarded the steamer, *Paul Jones,* for New Orleans. He had spoken his last words to James before leaving *Hurricane*. He would miss him. Their relationship over the years had bonded one to the other. Jeff knew he would lay down his life for the man, and he believed James felt the same way. The last night at the cabin, he had offered James his freedom. He promised to execute the document that very evening. Jeff was afraid that he might be killed in Mexico, and he wanted to be sure James would be protected if he did not return, but James declined the offer.

After Jeff had left for New Orleans, James wondered if he had made the right decision. His world had always been tied to the Davis family. The outside world was a fearful place. Perhaps if Jeff had made the offer earlier in his life, he would have accepted it. Now he was no longer a young man, and change had gotten harder as he grew older. The overriding reason, however, was that his wife and child were safe at *Brierfield*.

When their vessel docked in New Orleans, Jeff and Jim went immediately to the regiment's campground. As they approached the first person he recognized was his six-foot-seven-inch giant brother-in-law, Joseph Howell. Varina's tears over the war had not only been for Jeff. This brother was one she was very close to, and she feared for his safety as well. Another person he recognized was his favorite nephew, Robert, who had enlisted as a private. Soon they were surrounded by others who were from the Vicksburg and Natchez area.

That night, Jeff met with his two top commanders, Lieutenant Colonel McClung and Major Bradford. They had leadership qualities, and he personally liked them.

"The first order of business is to get the men out of this inclement weather," Jeff said. "The regiment needs shelter. Sleeping out in the open will only result in disease, death, and desertion."

"We've tried to get lumber to build shelter for them, but the wood yard the army has established here simply refuses our request," McClung said.

"Who's in charge there?" Jeff asked.

"Only a captain, but he thinks he's a general," Bradford said.

"Send one of our men to spy on the wood yard," Jeff said. "I want to know when the captain is not on duty."

Two days later Jeff struck. With two companies he approached the gate.

"Colonel Davis," Jeff announced, as he handed a requisition order to the sergeant of the guard.

"I'm sorry sir, but we have orders from the captain not to allow any material to be removed without his consent."

Do you dispute my rank or the terms of the order of requisition?"

"No sir."

"Then stand aside."

The sergeant and his men seemed hesitant to comply.

"McClung," Jeff said to his second in command, "this man is refusing to obey a direct order of his superior during a time of war. What should we do?"

"Shoot him."

The companies on signal raised their weapons. The color drained from the sergeant's face.

"That won't be necessary Colonel," he said. "Take whatever you want."

Jeff and his men marched through the gate and removed the materials they needed for the regiment.

In his first meeting with McClung and Bradford, Jeff had learned that Zachery Taylor was going to attack Mexico using the Brazos Island as a staging area on which to gather men and supplies. Word had been received from Taylor that Jeff's Mississippi Regiment would be leaving in a few days for this island, which lay near the mouth of the Rio Grande. Taylor was already on the Texas border with regiments of the regular army and was about to take the offensive against the Mexicans. During this same meeting with McClung and Bradford, Jeff had told them about the rifles and other equipment he had requisitioned for the regiment.

"That will make us the best armed regiment in the fight," McClung said.

"I expect them to arrive on the island before we are transported to the mainland," Jeff said.

When word spread among the troops, the men were pleased with the action of their colonel. This and the fact that upon his arrival he had arranged for their housing immediately made him popular. They felt he was concerned for their welfare. During the following week, ships transported the Mississippi Regiment to the island.

The port at Brazos was a good place to land, for it had the best natural occurring seaport in the Western Gulf. The island was the southernmost barrier island in Texas, and was of great commercial value to trade in the area. It was covered with sand dunes, low shabby vegetation, and a type of thin grass that was tolerant to salt.

Dear Varina,

Three days ago we arrived on Brazos Island. Most of the men are still suffering from sickness because of the rough seas we encountered. At the time we disembarked, no preparation in the way of housing had been made by the authorities. We have only been able to requisition tents for the officers. The men must, for the time being, sleep out in the open on the blankets they brought with them. There is very little in the way of permanent shelter on the island, and those are in a dilatory state having been constructed at various periods from the time the Spanish first set foot here. We are all hopeful that shortly we will be transported to the mainland.

I learned before departing New Orleans that General Taylor is planning an attack on Mexico. I hope that he will be pleased that I am in command of a volunteer regiment. Although, I'm not sure of his personal feelings toward me, I do believe that our estrangement was softened when we met by accident on the steamer.

Love,
Jeff

Despite the terrible conditions, Jeff trained his men daily. Complaints from the men reached his ears, but he chose to ignore them. He knew the soldiers were just raw recruits, and unless they learned discipline and elementary battle tactics, they would be slaughtered by any Mexican force they encountered.

Dear Varina,

The men are in a joyful mood today. Our rifles have arrived and much other equipment the regiment needs. Already everyone is calling our men The Mississippi Rifles, and I expect the name will stick.

There is other good news. A private message was received from General Taylor containing words of praise and expressing his desire to have me at his side. He has issued instructions to give my regiment priority, and we shall be the first to leave this godforsaken island. He is at Matamoros and is moving part of the army to Camargo. In the near future, we hope to be in battle and bring honor to our state and country.

Love,
Jeff

The regiment noticed that their commander walked with a new spring in his step and a show of confidence. They assumed it was the rifles, and the news they were being sent to the mainland soon. In truth, this did have a lot to do with the optimism Jeff felt. But it was also a letter from Taylor which had made him sure of his reception by his former father-in-law. Now Taylor had sent him a second private correspondence.

"I know from my personal observation of you as an officer at Fort Crawford that you are an able commander and that you will drill your men into an efficient unit. I need you by my side when I engage the enemy."

Taylor's letter also expressed concern about the politically appointed commanders with no military experience who were leading the raw recruits that composed the volunteer regiments.

After their arrival in Texas, Jeff left the regiment on August 24 and traveled on the steamer, *Virginia*, to Taylor's headquarters. He arrived on August 31 at Camargo, where he had a private meeting with the general. Over a drink neither mentioned the antagonism that previously existed between them, except for the general's comment that he regretted opposing the marriage. Their discussion centered on the present circumstances of the army, and his frustration with everything from the lack of supplies to the raw recruits that would soon comprise the majority of men under his command.

Taylor thought Jeff had aged considerably since the days when he was stationed at Fort Crawford. His hair had turned a solid gray, his figure appeared gaunt, and his left eye looked clouded while the right one cast a penetrating gaze. Jeff now had an aristocratic demeanor that made him seem distant and unapproachable.

When Jeff left Taylor's tent, he knew that his Mississippi Rifles would be in the Second Brigade, along with the First Tennessee under the command of General Quitman, a friend and neighbor on Davis Bend. Quitman owed his present rank to Jeff's political influence with President Polk in Washington.

* * *

Just two months after leaving New Orleans, the Mississippi Rifles were heading toward their first engagement with the enemy. Jeff was in his element in front of his men when they marched out of Camargo on September 7th toward Monterrey. He still wore civilian clothes because the uniforms he had been measured for in New Orleans had somehow been lost in transit and never arrived. Still, he looked impressive on his horse, Tartar.

The morning opened with the sun rising on a clear day. Jeff had camped his men in a wooded area near land that was filled with orchards and fields of corn, but this was not a day to linger and enjoy the view. The sound of artillery fire was already disrupting the quiet of the morning. Orders were delivered, and Jeff led his men out of the grove. He traveled on foot leaving behind Tartar in the care of Jim Green. General Quitman had directed Jeff to lead the Mississippi Rifles to the left of the Tennessee regiment. Soon he found himself marching between the Tennessee and Fourth U. S. Infantry. A lieutenant, Ulysses S Grant, for a brief moment observed this gaunt commander bravely leading his men forward into battle before his attention was diverted by Mexican artillery fire, and the view of solid cannon balls bouncing on the ground toward the oncoming troops.

"Watch out," Jeff warned his men as cannon balls came toward them.

One landed in front of Jeff with such force that after it hit the dirt, the ball bounced over his head and just missed a soldier following several yards behind. Despite the danger, Jeff felt no fear; his adrenaline pumping he continued to charge toward a fort called La Teneria. As they drew near, with musket shots whizzing past them and the mouth of Mexican cannons speaking loudly to them, Jeff shouted out his orders.

"Forward men, and don't fire until you can put your sights on them."

As they closed to within one-hundred-fifty yards, Jeff screamed above the noise of battle.

"Fire your rifles, and we shall put the enemy to flight."

Jeff led the men through an opening, waving his sword to encourage the men behind him. As he entered the fort, a rifle shot from the man on his left killed a Mexican soldier running toward him. A moment later he returned the favor by slashing at enemy soldiers charging out of a side alley.

The men were as pumped up as their commander. As the enemy ran out of the back of the fort to escape the Mississippians, Jeff and his troops gave chase until they were within sight of another fort protecting Monterrey, El Diablo. In their head long rush they may have taken it if Quitman had not appeared on horseback and ordered their retreat. That evening back at camp with the excitement over, Jeff got a report of his losses. The regiment had lost three officers. It had also suffered the death of seven enlisted men with forty-seven wounded. He felt compassion for the families they had left behind. His mind, however, could not dwell on this issue because he had received orders to continue the attack tomorrow. I must write a letter to Varina, he thought, for who knows what the next day might bring.

Dear Varina,

We fought our first battle today. The Mississippi boys performed well, and we were able to secure a great victory by capturing an enemy fort. I expect tomorrow will decide whether Monterrey will be ours.

An old friend visited our camp tonight. Albert Sidney Johnson, a friend from my West Point days, is attached to Taylor's headquarters. He has not yet received a regular commission, and is frustrated about it. He was given the command of a regiment of volunteers, but they had signed only a six month enlistment, and the men's time had expired. When it was put to a vote, the boys decided not to enlist for an extended period. The regiment dissolved and Sidney found himself without a command. What a pity, for I have always been impressed with his abilities. The government is making a big mistake by not offering him a command, since I believe he would be a brilliant commander if given the opportunity.

When I lead the charge tomorrow, I shall carry the lock of hair which you have sent me. It shall be placed upon my heart, for I feel the need to have your presence close to me.

Love,
Jeff.

* * *

The colonel and his men peered out from their position at the imposing El Diablo. There seemed to be no activity.

"Major Bradford, take a company and reconnoiter the area," Jeff said. "Be back within the hour for the attack will be coming soon."

In the semi-darkness, the men moved forward. Coming upon a knoll they observed campfires burning, but there were no soldiers about. It was apparent that the Mexican Army had slipped away in the night and left the fires to deceive the Americans, thus allowing the Mexicans to escape under cover of darkness. When Jeff received the word, he moved his men forward without waiting for orders. After passing through the confines of the fort, they entered the outskirts of Monterrey. Although the streets appeared deserted, soon the Mississippi Rifles came under intense fire from the rooftops and windows of buildings. The fighting became brutal as Jeff led his men in their first test of urban warfare. His men commented afterwards that it was amazing he was not killed, for he was often the first to enter a building making him the object of fire from the defenders.

By evening, it appeared that Monterrey would fall the next day. A white flag appeared on the horizon, and when Jeff saw it, he sent Bradford with a detachment to escort the Mexican officer to General Taylor's headquarters. Later, an aide to Taylor brought a message to Jeff as he sat beside a fire on which a piece of beef was being roasted by Jim Green.

Colonel Davis,
Please come to my tent posthaste. There are matters we need to discuss. Zack Taylor

"So you're going to see Old Rough and Ready," McClung said, using the nick-name commonly applied to the general, whose dress code often looked like that that of a recruit, and whose military career on the frontier had always shown him to be ready for action.

"I'll be back before dawn," he said to McClung. "Be sure the men are ready for tomorrow. We shall be victorious, but it may be bloody."

He mounted Tartar and rode off into the darkness toward Taylor's camp that was five miles away.

"Colonel Davis," Taylor said, "the Mexican General has asked for terms. If we can reach an agreement with him our victory will be secured without any further loss of life. I am going to appoint you on a commission of three to ride to his headquarters tomorrow morning and negotiate the terms."

"Who are the others?"

"General Worth and General Henderson."

When Jeff returned to his camp, he found Sidney sitting by the fire and sopping up beef and gravy with a biscuit.

"Hope you don't mind me coming over for supper. The army rations are getting old, and your man, Jim, has developed quite a reputation for creating some wonderful dishes out of whatever is available."

"You're always welcome. Has General Taylor secured you a federal command yet?

"No and I'm thinking of returning to my farm. The war will be over before I get my commission."

"I've been appointed on a committee to work out the terms of surrender with General Pedro de Ampudia tomorrow morning. Would you be willing to accompany me?"

"Hell, I might as well. I don't have anything else to occupy my time."

After Jeff had departed that evening, Taylor sat alone in his tent and drank some corn whiskey from a canister. He was beginning to feel his age, and often his mind was spent thinking about past events. Knoxie now seemed ever present in his thoughts. She had always been a daddy's girl. Their estrangement and then her death had scarred his soul deeply. Jeff's presence was probably one of the reasons her memory had been so vivid lately. She had loved the tall Mississippian so much that he now felt the need to look out for him. This did not take away from the fact that he thought Jeff was a fine officer. He had made an extra effort to put him in a position to win glory and thereby further his career.

That morning as the four American officers approached the Mexican lines under a white flag, they were nervous. Though there were some enemy regiments of high quality, many were made up of poor illiterate peasants. This element of the army saw the Americans as agents of the devil as their priest had called them. They reached the streets near the Grand Plaza without incident. From this position they observed armed infantry on the flat roofs and cannons in the middle of the streets. As they neared General Ampudia's headquarters, they were blocked by a small group of peasant soldiers who had all the attributes of a mob. Jeff was dressed in civilian clothes that had become quite ragged, and Sidney was wearing a red-flannel shirt, blue jeans, a torn checkered coat, and a wide-awake hat. The two generals' uniforms were tattered from wear.

The mob, because of their dress, thought they were Texans, which were to them the most despicable people. At this time, when they were in danger, a Mexican officer rode toward them. When they asked for his protection and guidance to headquarters, he gave them an evil smile and rode past them, after saying some words in Spanish that incited the mob into a frenzy. Sidney realized they were in great danger. He drew his pistol and rode up beside the Mexican officer. After placing the barrel to the man's temple, he took him hostage. This seemed to impress the mob that let them pass without further incident. In this fashion they arrived at the general's headquarters.

Jeff would write Varina the next day.

"The decisiveness of Sidney's actions by his quick thinking got us out of what was one of the most perilous situations of my life."

They were seated before General Ampudia and a select group of officers. General Worth presented the terms of surrender Taylor had written out. The general, who was fluent in the English language, read the terms to his officers. They engaged in much discussion in Spanish, while Jeff and the others sat quietly not understanding a word. However, the tone of the voices and the body language clearly showed that there was great disagreement not only over the terms, but also over the surrender itself. The general began to vacillate and then joined the other officers in opposing the terms of surrender. But after a passage of time, the Mexican officers had to concede they had no choice but to admit defeat.

At sunset copies of the negotiated terms that both sides accepted were executed by the parties. When they returned and handed General Taylor his copy, he read it in their presence. The agreement provided that the Mexican army would withdraw at least fifty miles, and Taylor would not advance for at least eight weeks. The Mexican Army would leave behind most of their field artillery and other armament, except that the officers were allowed to retain their horses and side arms and the enlisted men their arms and a limited amount of ammunition.

"You have done well," Taylor said to the three commissioners. "This agreement will prevent the further loss of American lives, and at the same time we have obtained our objective. The eight-week delay will also work to our advantage. Our men are exhausted, and our ammunition and food supplies have been depleted. This will give us time to replenish them."

When Jeff returned to his encampment there was a letter from Varina waiting for him. It was the third he had received this month. In the last two she had complained about Joseph and his family. This letter was no exception.

Dear Jeff,

Do not think that I am not worried about the danger that you must be facing every day in the Mexican Campaign, but I am facing a war of my own at Davis Bend. I have removed myself from Hurricane, and I am living once again at the cottage at Brierfield. The arrogance of your brother and the attitude of Eliza have driven me to this. I could no longer endure their attempts to control my every move and decision. I think you have relied too much in the past on Joseph's advice, and I do not think he always has your best interest at heart.

Need I remind you that the land upon which our home and cotton fields rest are still legally titled in his name. If something should happen to you, I shall not have an interest in anything that we have worked so hard to secure for our benefit.

If you do not come home soon, I will go back to Natchez and live with my parents who have been encouraging me to do so. As you know, my family has had recent disagreements with Joseph, and they no longer hold him in high esteem.

Do not think from the contents of this letter that I do not still have a high regard for you. I pray every day for your safe return, even though it may not be to my arms.

Love,
Varina.

The next day Jeff received a letter from Joseph explaining his side of the story, and informing Jeff that his wife was an immature woman who continually made poor judgments and refused on every occasion to follow his advice. Jeff knew he had to return to Mississippi to try to resolve the dispute that was threating his marriage and his relationship with his brother. He requested a furlough from General Taylor that was quickly granted. He addressed his regiment and promised them his visit home would be of short duration, and that he would be back with them before the next battle. Leaving McClung in command, he departed for Mississippi.

* * *

Jeff rode Tartar to Camargo accompanied by Jim Green, a person whom he had grown to respect for his service and the intellect that occasionally expressed itself. The two boarded a steamship, *Hatchee Eagle*, for the trip to Brazos Island. After a short delay on the island, the two men secured passage on a steamer that arrived in New Orleans on November 1. Although he had written both Joseph and Varina at Brazos Island that he was on his way to Davis Bend, he tarried for three days in the city. During this time, he once again arranged for a tailor take his measurements for a set of uniforms, the prior one having been lost and never recovered.

"I shall pay you in advance and do not desire that you forward it to me, for I shall pick it up upon my return to the city in a few weeks," he said to the tailor before depositing a sum of money in his hand.

He also purchased some other clothing, for his personal baggage was somewhat depleted, and the items of clothing that he still possessed were worn and damaged. Jim Green's trunk also was packed with new clothing, for Jeff felt that his man should not return home in tattered clothes.

On a steamer, Jeff and Jim sailed to Natchez where they spent the night. There, Jeff made a speech to a group of citizens who had gathered outside the hotel where they were staying. His talk was well received, and the next day they cheered him on his way when he and Jim boarded the ship for the rest of their journey.

Jeff had used the delays in his journey to muster the courage to face the turmoil he knew waited at home. He would have rather faced a hail of Mexican bullets. Their appearance at *Hurricane* sent a wave of excitement through the house, and the slaves came out of the fields to see Jeff. Word was sent to Varina by Joseph telling her that Jeff had landed.

"You should make haste," the note from Joseph said.

The slave that carried the message brought back a reply to Joseph. Varina would remain at the cottage at *Brierfield* and greet her husband there.

The two men retired to the library for a discussion before Jeff left for home. For the first time, Jeff learned that his brother had sent the resignation from Congress to the Speaker of the House.

"I didn't know at the time you would return so soon. You told me to hold it until I thought the war would last beyond the election season. It appears that it will, so I sent in your resignation."

The news had already made the papers, and candidates were already expressing an interest. Jeff was heartsick. He had hoped to be able to hold onto the seat, but Joseph was right. The war would last for some time, and he could not desert the Mississippi Rifles for a political campaign. After Jeff had a moment to absorb this information, Joseph poured out his heart about the family's problems with Varina. Then he advised Jeff to get his wife under control before it damaged him politically. Later that afternoon, Jeff swung into the saddle and turned Tartar toward *Brierfield*.

Varina had done her best to prepare the plantation to welcome its master home. The house slaves had cleaned until she was satisfied with the appearance of the home. A rider had been sent to Natchez to find James who had gone there to buy supplies. The slaves had gathered beneath the trees that lined the avenue that led to the house and already had begun to enjoy the food that Varina had the cooks prepare for them.

She had wanted everyone well fed and in a festive mood when the master of *Brierfield* rode down the avenue. Now Varina waited on the front porch impatiently and watched for his approach. For a moment she put aside the anger that still lay within her soul when she saw him coming down the avenue, and she went forth to meet him.

"I'm glad God has brought you safely home to me," she said.

When he dismounted, she embraced him and he felt relieved.

"I have missed you every day that I have been away."

"And I you."

The slaves gathered around Jeff. He spoke to each and embraced them individually. He truly had emotions for them and considered them part of his extended family. Many received his embrace with true affection, while others simply did what was expected by the rules of the society in which they had to survive. Varina and he then joined them at the wooden tables that had been set out beneath the trees, where they enjoyed laughter, conversation, and good food. When it grew dark, he bade them goodnight as they returned to their cabins.

Alone at last in the house, the two clung to one another, and their lips met in a passionate kiss. Without further conversation, she led him to the bedroom. Discarding any pretense of modesty, she removed the dress that her slave woman had created for the occasion. Having been faithful the long time he was away, Jeff was filled with lust for his alluring wife, and her faithfulness and youth had put her body in a state that it too desired immediate satisfaction. Soon the sexual tension between them was released.

The next morning, James came to the house and gave Jeff a short verbal report, and a longer accounting in writing, for James was more literate than the average white man in these parts. Before he could complete it, Jeff put his arms around him and held him close, for he had missed him.

The era of good feeling lasted only three days. When Jeff announced he was going to *Hurricane* to talk business with Joseph, Varina fell upon him with a fury.

"You value your brother's opinion over mine."

"That's not true."

"Where is the title to our plantation?"

Jeff did not respond, but instead started to leave the room.

"You know where it is. The property remains in your brother's name."

"He'll convey it to me."

"I doubt that."

As Jeff walked out onto the porch, she brought up a new bone of contention between them. The issue of a will entered into this one-sided conversation.

"I recently learned that Joseph has prepared a will for you," she said. "The document provides that upon your death I will receive only one-third of your estate with the rest of it left to your sisters, Anna and Amanda. You know this action will leave me for all practical purposes penniless since Joseph is sure to contest legal title to *Brierfield*. He is determined to make sure the Howells can never have a claim to property at Davis Bend. And I have learned when our new home is built, you plan to have Anna come and take up residence with us. You have never consulted me on this. You sometimes forget that I am your wife."

Varina then accused Jeff of not caring for her. It was not a good morning to say the least, and Jeff left earlier than planned for *Hurricane*, stating that he would spend the night there.

"In the morning when I return, I hope you will learn to control your tongue and act like a lady in the manner that society expects."

Those parting words did nothing to sooth her anger, and that day the letter she posted to her parents in Natchez would be received with sympathy. Though they had nothing against Jeff, she knew they felt Joseph was not treating her with the respect she deserved as a Howell.

When Jeff returned home that evening, the bickering continued. Varina reminded him that he promised her their present home would be temporary.

"When are you going to start construction of our mansion?" she asked.

He tried to appease her.

"As soon as the war is over."

"I will draw up the plans while you are away."

Varina then proceeded to lay out her vision of how she wanted the home constructed. Jeff, who fancied himself an architect, already had in mind his own ideas about how the house should be designed. When he tried to guide her in that direction, she resisted.

I don't have the finances, Jeff thought. My brother will have to provide the money. And if he does, Joseph will want input into the construction design. Jeff foresaw another conflict on the horizon as Joseph and Varina engaged in another struggle, with him being in the center trying to please both sides and able to please neither.

Jeff was anxious to return to Mexico. He cut his furlough short and with Jim Green at his side, he boarded a steamer at Davis Bend. Varina and Joseph with other members of his family saw him off. There was no embrace by his wife as he stepped aboard. After he had been home for three days, she had removed herself from his bed and spent the nights in the other bedroom. He had stayed the last night with James and his family. That same evening, he had presented his faithful servant, James, with his horse, Tartar, as a gift. He was a fine horse, but a message had arrived from Natchez two days ago that the citizens of that community planned to present him with a war horse named Richard. He looked forward to riding into battle dressed in a proper uniform upon such a fine stallion. He hoped such an appearance would inspire his troops.

When Jeff and Jim stepped off the boat at New Orleans they were met by an officer who had a message from the War Department. The uniforms for the Mississippi Rifles would be arriving in a few days. With them would also be bowie knives, which Jeff had persuaded President Polk to authorize for the unit. He was not disturbed by the need to delay his departure. Now that he was away from domestic turmoil, he could relax and enjoy the social life of the city where he had many acquaintances. He rented quarters for Jim and himself and tried to spend the time relaxing before he returned to war.

New Orleans had become a hub of military activity. Its depots were bulging with military hardware waiting shipment to the battlefronts. Regiments were arriving every day and encamping until transportation could be arranged to Mexico. The local aristocracy took this opportunity to entertain the officers. In addition, there were many wives who had taken residence in the city while they awaited their husbands' return from the war. Jeff immersed himself into the constant stream of parties. He cut a dashing figure in his new uniform, and the reputation he had earned at the Battle of Monterrey was well known. He basked in the attention he received, and the flirtation of the women restored his confidence in himself with the opposite sex. Perhaps, he thought, Varina does not appreciate me or that other women find me attractive. One night after an especially enjoyable evening, he wrote her the first letter since he had left home.

Dear Varina,
I am still in New Orleans having received notice that the uniforms for the Mississippi Rifles will arrive at the port very soon. I felt that I should take possession of them lest they get misplaced in transit as so often happens in these matters.

The social life has been quite lively, and I must say that I have renewed acquaintances with many lovely ladies who for various and sundry reason have taken up residence in the city for the duration of the war. When you are in an introspective mood, I hope this information will furnish food for contemplation.

Your husband,
Jeff

By the time Varina received the letter, Jeff and Jim had departed the city, and were on their way to Mexico with the uniforms and bowie knives. Varina bristled when she first read the communication from her husband. She immediately gave orders to her house slave to pack her clothes.

"I'm going to visit my parents in Natchez, and I want you to accompany me."

Not wanting to communicate with Joseph, she found out by other means when the next steamer would be docking at Davis Bend. She was pleased to learn that a boat headed toward Natchez would be arriving the next day.

* * *

Varina's parents were surprised to see her, having received no advanced warning that she was coming.

"I just need a break from *Brierfield*," she said. "It can be so boring, and there's no social life."

Varina's father accepted this, but her mother suspected there were more reasons for the visit then her daughter was disclosing. Two days after her father left for Vicksburg on business, Varina exploded with an outburst of words describing the situation at Davis Bend, and the problems she was having in her marriage.

"Dear," her mother said, "can't you see that Jeff's letter was simply an attempt to make you jealous? If he didn't care, he would not have put that information about other women into his letter. Now you treated him poorly the few days he was home at *Brierfield*. I suspect that's why he returned to Mexico so soon. We received a letter from your brother, John, who said he didn't expect Colonel Davis back for another month."

"I didn't realize he left before he had to, Mama."

"You must remember that he is a national hero whose star may continue to rise. As a woman, you have no place if you are not at his side, even if you don't love him."

"But I do love him," she said in protest, though at the moment she wasn't sure of her feelings that were in a state of turmoil.

"Then you must suppress some of the hostility you are constantly expressing to him. Write him a letter expressing your love. And do it right away."

"But what about Joseph? I've told you how we just can't get along, and he doesn't like father anymore."

"Now honey, you must realize that is not totally Joseph's fault. Your father is a good man, but his business dealings are sometimes highly suspect. To Joseph, honestly and integrity are very important. There's something else that I am going to confide in you. It is a very personal thing. Joseph and I were very close at one time. And I mean very close. I don't think your father realized that until recently when Joseph reprimanded him about putting my social status in jeopardy. You see, there are a lot of dynamics going on here that are having a negative impact on your marriage."

"I didn't realize."

"There's one more thing you must consider. You and Joseph are both jealous of Jeff's affection. Your husband is in the middle. Don't make him choose between a brother, who really is more like a father, and his wife. Even if you win the contest, he will resent you for it."

Alone that night in a bedroom Varina had claimed as her own while growing up in a household filled with brothers, she thought over what her mother had said. In her mind there formed a plan. She would make peace with Joseph and learn to share Jeff's affections. Tonight she would reach out to Jeff by writing the type of letter her mother had proposed. And before his return, she would try to sort out her feelings toward him.

My Darling Jeff,
I have missed you so and regret the way I treated you on your last visit. When you return, I shall embrace you and prove to be a good wife. In trying to find the maturity you seek in a spouse, I have started reading a book given to me by my mother titled, *The Guide To Social Happiness*. I'm glad you enjoyed your stay in New Orleans and expect by the time this letter is received, you will be back with the regiment.
God Bless and Keep you Safe,

Your loving wife,
Varina

He received his wife's letter while waiting at Brazos Island for transportation to Mexico. He posted an immediate response.

My Dear Varina,

I received your letter today, and your expression of love brought me great comfort. I'm glad to see that you are studying ways to improve yourself as a wife. You are young, and it is not fair for me to expect with so little experience in life, you could have already obtained the insight that your much older husband has had the advantage of finding. You must seek to rise above petty annoyances and strive to avoid collisions with those you love. Finding a happy state is not always obtained by being so determined to steer an independent course that you abandon the conventional role of a spouse.

I have thought of your vision for our new home. Make whatever plans you desire, and I shall yield to you on this matter and construct it according to your wishes. For it must be so if we are to find a measurement of happiness within its walls.

I miss you terribly and hope to return to your loving arms, soon.

Keeping you always in my thoughts,
Jeff

* * *

The return trip to Taylor's army was slowed because Jim had to drive a wagon with the military gear for the regiment. It took weeks to reach Montemorelos where Taylor had located his headquarters.

Jeff joined the general and his staff for dinner on Christmas Day. The officers complimented Jeff on his regiment which had passed in review before the general's tent that morning. The Mississippi Rifles were the envy of the others at headquarters as they now appeared dressed in red shirts, white duck trousers, and black hats with bowie knives in sheaths attached to their belts.

"Jeff," the general said in a private conversation after the other officers had left the tent on Christmas evening, "I plan a winter campaign. We will march on Victoria, but keep this to yourself. It will be a few days before I let the other regimental commanders know of my plans. It is important that we take the capital of Tamaulipas and place our men deep in the heart of the province before Santa Anna reaches it. I fear we shall be greatly outnumbered from the reports I have been receiving. We may soon be facing thousands of enemy troops.

"Unfortunately, I've have had to send some of our best units to General Scott, who is preparing an attack on Veracruz. We are reduced to less than 5,000 men. They even took General Quitman and his brigade, but I insisted that they detach the Mississippi Rifles from the brigade and leave them under my command. You are one of my best commanders, and you have trained the regiment so well, that they perform like regular troops."

"Thank you for the compliment. I shall do all that I can in the coming conflict to prove that your confidence has not been misplaced."

The men were excited when word came down that the army was to march. They had become bored with camp life and looked forward to action again. Jeff felt the same. He was anxious to defeat the enemy, bring glory to his regiment, and prove his courage in battle.

On the way to Victoria, General Taylor and members of his staff approached Jeff as he was leading his men forward. Seeing Taylor at a distance, Jeff put McClung in command and rode back to meet him. Much to his surprise, Robert E. Lee was among the officers with the general. Jeff had not seen him since their days at West Point, but the two had corresponded on an infrequent basis.

"How's your regiment doing?"

"Very well, General. Their health is good and their spirits are high."

"Let me introduce you to Captain Robert E Lee. He's an engineer attached to my command."

"I know the captain," Jeff said. "We were at West Point together."

Then turning to Lee he said, "Robert, if you get a chance, stop by my tent tonight, and we can reminisce about old times at the academy."

"I'd love to," Lee said.

"Unfortunately, this will be his last day with us," the general said. "He has orders to leave tomorrow and join General Scott's expedition. They are not going to be satisfied until they get all my regulars and leave me with nothing but the volunteers."

Jeff was not offended by the remark, because he knew his regiment was held in high esteem by the general.

The provincial troops were gone by the time the American army reached Victoria. They had been ordered to leave and join General Santa Anna at La Encarnacion. Jeff was riding beside his commander when the mayor and his council rode out to meet them and surrender the city without resistance. After establishing American authority in the area, the general returned to Monterrey. While he was organizing his resources, word reached him that the Mexican forces were on the move. He quickly marched to Saltillo where he expected the main attack would come.

They had been in Saltillo only a few hours when he ordered his men to continue their march to Agua Nueva where he planned to set his base camp. But before he reached it, a dispatch rider brought information from one of the outpost he had established. Santa Anna was moving toward him with an army of 20,000 men.

"Jeff," he said to his favorite colonel who was riding beside him when he received the information, "we shall not have time to fortify Agua Nueva. I will have the men in the outposts retreat to Buena Vista. The hill country there gives Santa Anna little choice on his approach. He must move his troops by way of the San Luis Potosi Saltillo road. There is a narrow place along the way called La Angostura where the Mexican

Army's movement will be greatly restricted. That will reduce the advantage they have in numbers."

"Like Leonidas against the Persians at the Thermopylae Pass," Jeff said.

"We will at least be able to delay their advance. I still believe the decisive battle will be fought at Saltillo."

The army evacuated their base at Agua Nueva just before the arrival of the Mexican Army. An American cavalry unit that stayed behind burned wagonloads of supplies just before the first wave of enemy cavalry arrived. The Americans beat a hasty retreat, but kept their unit between the advancing Mexicans and Taylor's retreating troops. In doing so, they fought several skirmishes until the enemy cavalry broke off the battle and returned to their main body. By that evening the American army had traveled fifteen miles to the north and reached the Buena Vista hacienda.

After giving orders on where he wanted the troops positioned, Taylor returned to Saltillo. He took Jeff and the Mississippi Rifles with him. Once he arrived he began issuing orders and laying out his plan to defend it.

"General," Jeff said, "don't you think our cause would be better served if you allowed me to return to Buena Vista with my men?"

"Colonel Davis, your regiment has the only experienced veterans. You will form the core of any defense, offense or reserve. Do you understand?"

Jeff ignored the sharpness in the general's voice. He knew the general had spent two days without sleep, and it was beginning to wear on him as it would any man his age.

"I want to serve wherever I can be of the most use to you," Jeff responded.

The next morning as the general and Jeff were drinking coffee and discussing what should be given priority that day, a message arrived. Santa Anna had moved quickly and was now near Buena Vista. Under a flag of truce, he had delivered to an American outpost a demand that Taylor surrender his entire army. Within the hour the two men were riding hard toward Buena Vista to stiffen the backbone of the regiments in place and to send the Mexican General, Taylor's response.

Upon arriving, Taylor read the Mexican demand.

"You are surrounded by twenty thousand men, and cannot avoid a rout and being cut to pieces. I wish to save you from a catastrophe. I therefore demand the surrender of your army. You will be granted an hour's time to make up your mind. After that, I shall order my men to attack."

Taylor dictated a reply, which Jeff wrote down and handed to a staff officer to deliver under a white flag to the enemy.

"In reply to your note of this date, summoning me to surrender my forces, I beg leave to say that I decline acceding to your request."

Almost immediately after the response reached Santa Anna's hands, the Mexican general sent orders to his regimental commanders and skirmishes between some of the forward units began. In the meantime, the Mississippi Rifles were on the road from Saltillo marching at a fast pace with their supply wagon following at a great distance. They were reunited with their colonel by noon. Both were anxious to move forward to where they could already hear the sounds of battle, but Taylor held them in reserve because he still did not have a clear view of Santa Anna's strategy. By evening there had not been a major thrust by the enemy, and Taylor decided to ride back to Saltillo before darkness fell. He ordered Jeff to accompany him. The Mississippi Rifles encamped at Buena Vista in the rear of the other American regiments.

"I still believe we will fight the major engagement at Saltillo," he said to Jeff as they galloped in that direction.

When they arrived, Taylor and Jeff worked feverishly at the defenses and instructed the officers on the placement of their troops should American troops be forced to retreat from Buena Vista. As day was breaking, Jeff accompanied Taylor back to the battlefield. The Mississippi boys gave a cheer when they saw the two riding in their direction.

Jeff gave his first order of the day. "Get the men in formation. We will be escorting the general to the front."

Jim Green appeared with a rifle. He had begged Jeff to let him fight at his side. Many of the Mississippians had brought their personal body servants with them, and they had fought beside their masters in earlier engagements. Jeff could not deny his man the same opportunity.

The regiment moved out double-quick just behind the general. They covered the six-mile distance to the front in less than two hours. A short time after the General had departed, they could hear the roar of cannon fire. Soon the sounds of small arm fire also filled the air. Jeff pushed his men forward giving them no respite except to stop at a small stream to fill their canteens with water. Soon they came into contact with the Second Indiana Volunteers who had broken rank in the face of a cavalry charge that had hundreds of Mexican infantry following in their wake. Jeff rode forward on his horse, Richard, through the fleeing men, waving his sword. "The enemy is that way. Follow me."

As Jeff and his Mississippi regiment charged forward with a shout of victory or death, the volunteers rallied and joined them. Bullets whistled over their heads and around them, but the men continued their charge. On the horizon appeared a line of enemy cavalry, followed by infantry. Jeff had the men fall into battle order and then once again commenced the advance. He realized that if the enemy was successful here, they could seize the road to Saltillo and cut off the Americans from their supply base, trapping them in the desert without provisions.

"Hold your fires, boys," he said.

Jeff hoped to get close enough to release a deadly volley into the mass of men that was drawing ever closer. Then as it seemed the tide of humanity was going to overwhelm them, the command to fire burst from his lips. The enemy stopped, and when a second volley spit forth, it wavered. At the third volley, the Mexican formation simply disintegrated. The enemy began to flee back toward their own lines. Jeff's men and the Indiana volunteers moved onward at a quick pace, keeping up a steady fire.

"Colonel, you've been hit," Jim said.

In the excitement of the moment, Jeff had not felt the impact of the musket ball that struck his right foot and drove bits of brass spur, boot, and stocking deep into his instep, shattering the bone. Now suddenly, the pain became excruciating, but he refused several offers of help. Instead, he took a handkerchief from his pocket, bound the injury to slow the bleeding, and remained in the saddle. Finally, realizing his men were too far out in front of the American lines, he ordered a retreat. As they began to move back toward their own lines, he saw enemy cavalry in the distance trying to cut off his retreat. As the cavalry passed through a ravine, he led the men, who were within the sound of his voice, to the ravine's edge. They poured a withering fire at the horsemen who were now at a temporary disadvantage, and put them to flight, thereby saving his regiment from annihilation.

The Mississippi Rifles were now without ammunition. Jeff immediately sent word back to the supply base for more. It arrived, but to their dismay there was a mix-up. The men discovered the cartridges were of a larger caliber and could not be loaded into their rifles. Still mounted and with blood dripping from his wound, Jeff instructed the men to take rocks and to hammer the bullets to reduce their diameter. It worked, but although they could now fire, its effect was to reduce their accuracy to no better than muskets. Right after they completed this work, the American line in their sector was again subjected to an attack by the enemy cavalry in another attempt by the Mexicans to seize the road to Saltillo. Jeff marched his men forward and put them into battle formation. As the cavalry approached within range, Mexican cannons began to pound the American position. Soon the solid shots were hitting the ground around their position. By riding up and down in front of his troop, Jeff kept them in place. As the cavalry came within range, his troops' fire emptied enough saddles to cause the enemy once again to withdraw. In the midst of this action Taylor appeared. After the Mexicans fled the field, he complimented Jeff on the action of his men, and then rode off to inspect other positions that were under attack.

An hour later, after receiving new supplies of the correct ammunition, he ordered his men to advance once again. As they came near the ravine where the earlier fire fight had taken place, two thousand enemy cavalry suddenly appeared and swept toward them across the flat piece of land as the Mississippi and Indiana boys were marching forward. Jeff knew the men were outnumbered three to one, but retreat would result in the American flank collapsing and the army's defeat. As the cavalry charged, he realized that the usual formation in a hollow square as Wellington had used at Waterloo would not work because there were too many cavalry, and he had too few soldiers. So he directed them into a V-shape formation.

As the enemy got closer, the Americans could see the Mexican commander on a white horse. The men following him were all handsomely dressed and riding beautiful horses. They represented the crème of the Mexican army.

Jeff rode Richard up and down the line. He ignored the fact that this made him an easy target to enemy snipers and encouraged his men to be brave. As the cavalry came closer, he ordered them to hold their fire knowing that he must lure the enemy into the trap he had set for them.

"Hold you fire, men, until they get close."

They obeyed him and waited in complete silence. At the last moment Jeff removed himself from their line of fire.

"Fire and then at them with your knives."

He added the last part of the order because he wasn't sure whether the first round would break their charge, and the men might not have time to reload. The Mexican general did not see the genius of Jeff's plan, and he led the charge right into the V-trap. In a few minutes the ground was littered with dead men and horses. The air was filled with the cries of enemy wounded.

No sooner had this great victory been won than Jeff received orders to aid the right flank that was about to be overrun.

"Re-form the men," he shouted and began moving in that direction.

The ground on this part of the battlefield was hilly, and Jeff could see only a few yards ahead. Just as he reached a plateau, a large contingent of enemy infantry came into view. Though his men were outnumbered, he formed them into a battle line just in time to meet the assault.

"We are going to be overwhelmed," Jeff said to Jim, who was beside him. "The numbers are just too great."

At the very last moment, Captain Braxton Bragg came to their rescue. He arrived with three pieces of flying field artillery and set up a position several hundred yards away. He and his men were in great personal danger for there was no infantry to support them. As the Mexicans charged Jeff's men, the American artillery rounds landed among them. Between the exploding shells and the regiment's fire, the enemy broke and ran. Jeff would never forget the courageous action of Bragg, and he would forever feel a debt of gratitude. Without Bragg's action, Jeff knew his men would have been wiped out. There would still be actions by other units later that day, but for all practical purposes Jeff's actions had assured Taylor a victory.

As soon as the attack was over, Jeff almost fell off his horse. The loss of blood had caused him to begin to lose consciousness. Jim saw what was happening and helped him dismount. A nearby wagon was secured, and Jeff, attended by Jim, was taken to a field hospital in the rear.

General Taylor upon hearing of this, came to visit him once the fighting had stopped that evening.

"I'm glad you are just wounded," the general said.

The first reports he had received were that his favorite colonel had been killed in action.

"I shall be able to return to duty tomorrow," Jeff said, his lips quivering from the pain.

Taylor looked at the pale man lying on the cot before him and knew this war was over for him, but he felt the need to comfort him.

"I don't think that will be necessary. The Mexicans are beaten. I would not be surprised if we don't receive a message from Santa Anna in the morning.

"What were our casualties?" Jeff asked.

"We suffered heavy losses. Perhaps the dead number as high as seven hundred men. We are also getting low on ammunition and other supplies."

After Taylor left the tent, he dispatched an order putting McClung in command of the Mississippi Rifles, and ordered them placed at the front where the enemy might attack the next day, if Santa Anna decided he still stood a chance of dislodging the Americans.

The next morning Jeff awoke determined to lead his troops. Finding that he could not mount his horse, he had Jim secure a wagon to take him to the regiment's location so that he could encourage them in the battle that might surely come that day. But there was no battle. Santa Anna had had enough. A scouting party reported to General Taylor that the Mexicans had slipped away during the night.

* * *

The sun shone through the bedroom window at *Brierfield*. Jeff lay there in the stillness of the morning only half-awake. Then the sound of feet rushing about the house reached his ears as Varina gave orders to the staff. Soon there will be hot coffee and biscuits delivered to my room, he thought. This is certainly a more pleasant environment than the hospital at Monterrey.

Jeff had spent a month in an army field hospital after the battle of Buena Vista. He was treated there by doctors who wanted to avoid amputating his foot, and they had been successful in saving it, but now he was on crutches and would need to continue using them for the next two years. His own physician from Natchez said he would suffer great pain for a long time from his wound, as the foreign matter worked its way out of his flesh.

Varina followed her kitchen girl down the hallway to Jeff's room. This was the daily routine that had been established. She would join Jeff while he ate breakfast, and they would have their morning talk. Afterward, Jeff would sit on the front porch and read while she supervised the household staff and her gardener. Sometime before noonday, James would come and discuss with Jeff the progress of agriculture projects on the plantation. At the end of each day after they had retired to their bedroom, Varina would read to him, and on occasion, he would dictate some letters, which she would have delivered to the next steamer that docked.

At first, Varina was content just to have her husband home again. *Brierfield* could be a lonely place when your only companions were slaves who had lives she could never be part of because of the social order. Her isolation at the plantation while Jeff was in Mexico had even driven her to stay at *Hurricane* a few weeks after he had left to return to military duty the last time. There she had tried her best to reconcile with Joseph. He had also reached out to her in an attempt to heal the ever-widening breach between them. They had achieved partial success, but before Jeff came home, she had once again fled *Hurricane* and returned to *Brierfield* where she had kept busy by supervising the creation of a flower garden that surrounded three quarters of her home.

Upon Jeff's return, she attended numerous public receptions given in his honor as a war hero and other social gatherings. It had been so thrilling initially, and Varina had basked in the shadows of his glory. That time had now passed, and the boredom of everyday life at *Brierfield* had returned. It was not easy living with an older man who had excruciating pain, used crutches, and suffered other health problems such as bouts of malaria, and inflammation of his eye. It was about to drive her mad. She tried to be a good wife, but she wanted more out of life. Soon they began to quarrel again.

When the discord worsened Varina escaped by fleeing to her parents' home in Natchez for several weeks. Added to her marital stress were the arguments over the construction on their new home. Despite his promise, Jeff did not give her complete control of designing the house. He was insistent that it be breezy and comfortable. If she heard those two words again, she felt she would scream. She became so distraught over things that she became ill and took to bed for two weeks. The doctors gave her some medication, and eventually this helped her nerves to recover enough that she was able to resume supervising the household. She wrote a letter to a friend in Natchez during this period.

"My unhappiness continues. During the months of my marriage, Jeff has been away either campaigning or fighting. I am twenty-one and have not yet had a child, and wonder if I am barren. What should become of me if I cannot bear him children, for he wants to have a large family? Life is not as I expected it to be. My dreams of living the life of a planter's wife with social gatherings, surrounded by a loving husband, and family have not come to fruition. Sometimes I doubt that it ever will happen. I am afraid that my youth and my dreams are fast slipping away, and that I am powerless to change the course of my life."

THE SENATOR

As the conflict between Jeff and Varina continued, an event occurred which changed their lives and put Jeff on a course that would give him an opportunity to make his mark upon the history of his nation. The United States Senator from Mississippi died, and Jeff was appointed by the governor to fill his unexpired term. This came on the heels of his rejection of a commission offered by President Polk that would have made him a brigadier general of new volunteers regiments formed for duty with the occupation forces in Mexico. He had wanted to accept it, but his view of the constitution forbade it. With regrets he had penned a letter of response to the president.

"I am greatly honored by your offer. It is with great sorrow that I must decline the same. Under my view of the constitution, the power to appoint officers for volunteers resides with the governor of a state."

With this rejection, his life would now center on politics and public office. Thoughts of a military career were now behind him.

The time for departure for Washington on a steamer was set for November 11ᵗʰ. Jeff trembled inside as he prepared to tell his wife that she would not be accompanying him to Washington. He knew their marriage was in trouble, and that the marital discord that was hidden from public view in the isolation at *Brierfield* would be exposed if they lived together at the capital. He chose a moment when they were sitting on the front porch one evening after the servants had retired for the night.

"Varina, I have decided not to take you to Washington."

"Why?"

"We need time apart."

"You always make decisions without consulting me. We have spent most of our marriage apart, and it certainly hasn't helped."

"I have overlooked a lot of your conduct because you are young and inexperienced in life. But if your attitude doesn't change, your conduct shall render it impossible for us to ever live together again."

"Don't talk to me in such a condescending way. You think you know everything."

"There you go with that attitude. Now don't throw a temper tantrum."

"Don't speak to me like a child. I'm your wife."

"Then start acting like one."

Varina left the porch in a huff and went into the house.

I used poor judgment in marrying her, he thought. I'm too old to deal with her foolishness. She just doesn't show me the respect she should. I led men in battle, served in the House, and now I'm going to be a United States Senator. Why can't she just grow up and listen to me. In disgust, he walked down to James' home, and that night he slept in a recently built spare bedroom.

As he was preparing to go to Washington, he received a correspondence from his friend Armistead Burt.

"Have you heard about Congressman Abraham Lincoln's 'Spot of Blood' speech? Even his fellow Whigs are appalled. Questioning the war when we are on the way to total victory is unpatriotic. If he had the votes, it would be the end of Manifest Destiny. Much of the West would have remained under Mexican control, and the British eventually would have controlled California to keep the Russians out. We would be blocked from the Pacific Ocean, except for Oregon. He may have the same disease as his father, Calhoun, but definitely not his foresight or his political skill. I understand that he will not file for another term because he can't win."

When he arrived in Washington, Jeff rented quarters at Gadsby's on Pennsylvania Avenue. The next day he paid a visit to President Polk at the executive mansion. He assured the president of his support for the Democratic presidential candidate, despite his close personal relationship with Taylor, who was the Whig candidate. Afterwards, he went to the Senate where he was sworn in by the Vice President. Although a freshman, he was given great notice as the only veteran of the Mexican War that sat in the chamber.

The unexpired term was a short one, though Jeff had taken it in the belief that the legislature would elect him to a full term the next year. Soon word reached him that his fellow senator from Mississippi, Henry Foote, was working behind the scenes to have a political ally elected to the seat. Not long afterwards, when he was in a public room of the hotel where members would gather in the afternoon for drinks, Foote confronted Jeff over his opposition to the Missouri Compromise. Jeff, never one to back down from an argument or fight, ridiculed his argument. Thinking he could intimidate Jeff, who only weighed 140 pounds, Foote who was a big man got up in Jeff's face. Jeff swung the first punch which landed on Foote's jaw. They began punching each other, and it took several congressmen to pull them apart. More words were spoken and Jeff challenged Foote to a duel. Some of Jeff's friends convinced him to withdraw the challenge. When he went to his quarters, he sat down at his desk and composed a letter to his friend, Sidney Johnson, explaining his confrontation with Foote.

"It should not have happened. I am not well and am ill-tempered living alone in this room far from my home and family."

On January 11, 1848, the Mississippi Legislature elected Jeff to a full term. This gave him new confidence, and he decided to make some positive changes in his life. He started by moving from Gadsby's Hotel to a boardinghouse. He also buried himself in his duties as a member of the military affairs committee and the board of regents for the Smithsonian. The few letters he received from Varina did not give him comfort. They only spoke of his perceived shortcomings and her unhappiness. His letters to her were not uplifting either, as he recounted what he saw as her defects in being a good wife. This domestic drama continued as Jeff poured himself into his senatorial duties.

Jeff began to speak out in the Senate on issues that were important to him. In a short time, he was becoming a national figure. The public was interested in this war hero who stood in second place only to Taylor, for his service in the Mexican War.

As the Senate neared adjournment, only one issue remained. The issue of slavery raised its ugly head over the status of Oregon. In the past, new states had been allowed after they organized to decide whether or not to allow slavery. Now, the North wanted Oregon to be denied to slaveholders while it was still a territory. It struck Jeff as wrong to restrict any American's right to take his property into a territory. Such action would make Southerners second-class citizens.

From the floor of the Senate, he spoke against such a concept.

"This will destroy political equality. I am afraid that where the states have in the past lived in harmony as partners, they will now increasingly find one another's company intolerable. The issue is not slavery, but the beginning of a struggle for political power between sections of this country. If allowed to go on unabated, the national political parties will find their natural constituents broken, and a sectional party will arise that will seize power and deprive other sections of their rights. Oppression by the majority will become the rule of the day."

Jeff's constitutional concepts were not formed as an excuse to defend slavery. Though later as things heated up, the concepts of states' rights would be used as a defense of the South's peculiar institution. In a letter to a friend in Ohio, he set forth his views.

"I do feel that as a culture, the Negro is inferior. This is a view held by American citizens throughout the United States and by the civilization in Europe from which our ancestors immigrated."

Strangely, Jeff had spent more time in the North during his life than the South. Until he was elected President of the Confederacy, he never visited the cotton states beyond Mississippi, except for the trips he made to New Orleans. Nor had he visited the upper southern states of Virginia and North Carolina. His view of slavery consisted primarily of Davis Bend, where James was as close to him as a brother and ran his plantation, just as Ben Montgomery ran *Hurricane*. His world in Mississippi was a place where literacy was encouraged, and entrepreneurship was promoted.

In August the Congress recessed as usual because the temperature in the congressional building became too warm. He prepared to return home and worried about what type of reception waited him. Varina and he had not corresponded for two months. Except for the brief note he had sent notifying her about the date when Congress would adjourn, and the week he expected to arrive back at *Brierfield*.

* * *

Varina's mood was positive, and she felt a certain amount of optimism about life. This feeling arose from many things. The coming of spring brought the blossoming of flowers. This had always lifted her spirits even as a child. And last week Joseph had come to her home and spent the day. They had visited the site where the *Brierfield* mansion would be built. Afterwards, over the mid-day meal, she had discussed with him her dreams about the structure, where Jeff and she would at last have a suitable place to live and entertain. Joseph had been receptive, and he had not made any remarks that might have dampened her enthusiasm for the project. When he left, she felt relieved. Her thoughts turned to the news that Jeff would be returning soon. Perhaps this time, they would be able to make their marriage work. She was willing to give it another try.

Jeff was happy. Varina had met him at the boat with Joseph and his family. They had spent the night at *Hurricane* and the next day ridden *to Brierfield*. Stacked under the sheds was building materials that had arrived over the last few weeks. And Joseph had promised the use of several of his slaves to aid in the construction of the home. That evening as they discussed their plans for the house, their joint enthusiasm overrode any differences on its design. They shared the same bed and when Jeff woke the next morning, he heard Varina singing in the kitchen. He was determined to make it a good day.

Jeff had been home three weeks, and things were going well both in the construction of the new home and in their marriage. Varina took this opportunity to write a positive letter to a friend in Natchez.

"I feel alive again. All my melancholy has disappeared. Jeff has been wonderful, and he seems genuinely happy to be back at *Brierfield*.

"The construction of our new home is progressing at a fast pace. It will be a one-story house with two large rooms on opposite sides of the hallway in the center of the house. As you enter from the front porch, on the right is a library and on the left a parlor. The bedrooms will be at the rear of the house. Behind the home in a separate structure is the kitchen.

"I hope when it is finished, you will come and stay a few days."

Jeff stayed with Varina for two months before he returned to Washington.

"I will miss you, my love," she had whispered in his ear the night before he departed.

"I wish you could come with me," he had replied before kissing her.

The words that were spoken were sincere. The two had discussed her going to the capital with him, but they agreed that Varina needed to stay at *Briarfield* to keep a careful eye on the construction.

As Jeff waved to Varina from the steamer, he was content with his marriage. It had been a pleasant visit. The only dark cloud that appeared on the horizon during the two months was with Joseph. His brother thought Varina's house plans costs too much, and he suggested they scale them back. Jeff had sided with his wife which pleased her, but it irritated Joseph.

Joseph watched from the landing as the steamer departed. His relationship with Jeff had cooled during his stay. To avoid problems with Varina, he had withdrawn his objection to her house plans. It was going to cost a lot of money. The sum necessary for the construction was totally financed by him. He wondered if Jeff would ever be able to pay him back. His desire to have his brother close had required many loans over the years. None had been paid, not even the first one for the ten slaves purchased. However, Jeff now had four hundred acres in production. Most of it was in cotton. If things continued, his brother would soon have enough wealth to satisfy his debts.

* * *

When Jeff returned to Washington, the first fire storm over slavery was being ignited by a man who was often referred to as the Great Compromiser. Henry Clay, in trying to resolve the issue of slavery, introduced the Omnibus Bill. His good intentions backfired, and for the first time in the nation's history slavery was on the front burner of political debate.

"This bill will abolish the slave trade in the District of Columbia, settle the boundary between Texas and New Mexico, and admit California as a free state, while leaving the issue of slavery to be decided by the New Mexico Territory and Utah Territory after their admission as states," Clay said. "In addition, I have included a provision requiring the federal government to assist in returning run-away slaves to their masters."

The bill was meant to appease all factions, but it pleased no one. From the start of the debate, Jeff became the new Calhoun as he rose to speak in defense of the Southern position. From this point on, he became the leader that the South looked to in Congress to defend their cause. Calhoun was there, but he just sat and encouraged the new lion. He could no longer rise from his seat without assistance. He was dying. Things became so heated that Delaware offered a petition calling for the peaceful dissolution of the Union. Jeff was on his feet to argue against it.

"The Congress has no right to dissolve our Union. Under our constitution only the states have that right. And God forbid that it should ever come to that. We must remember the blood that was shed by our fathers and grandfathers for this remarkable republic that the states formed. We are a nation that gives hope to the rest of mankind, most of whom live in darkness under the rule of despots."

Slavery itself, Jeff would not attempt to defend on the floor of the Senate. When the issue was raised in argument on the justification for it, he had a standard reply. In his personal life he followed the teachings of Jesus who said a master should be kind to his slave, and in return a slave should obey his master.

"It is enough for me that it is established by decree of the Almighty God, and sanctioned in the Bible, in both Testaments, from Genesis to Revelation."

His view was simply a statement of the prevailing theological view that had always been prevalent in the Western world, though it was beginning to erode.

When the Congress took a recess, Jeff hurried home anxious to see Varina again. Back at *Brierfield*, the construction of the house was proceeding, and Jeff was satisfied with what had been accomplished under Varina's supervision. When it came time to return to the capital, he could not bear to leave her. She felt the same way. They decided she would accompany him and spend a month in Washington before returning. In the meantime construction would stop; neither trusted Joseph and the slaves to complete the task to their satisfaction without Varina's presence.

Varina first heard of the duel in the lobby of the hotel where they were staying. When Jeff returned from the Senate that day she confronted him about it.

"Is it true that you have challenged Congressman Bissell to a duel?"

"He disrespected the honor of the Mississippi Rifles."

"You could be killed."

"It's a matter of honor."

"I just don't understand. This is the fifth time you have issued a challenge. How could you constantly put me at risk of being a widow?"

"Dueling should be the last resort of a gentleman. But sometimes it is the only way to defend one's name. In this case, I was their colonel, and I am defending the honor of all the men who served in the regiment."

She left the room in disgust, thinking how foolish men were to kill over perceived slights. Two days later she was happy to hear that the matter between Bissell and her husband had been resolved through intermediaries.

Varina would be leaving Washington soon to return to *Briarfield*. She hated to go. The social life and the times she had sat in the Senate Gallery and watched the work of that body were fascinating.

One day while Varina stood near the entrance to the Senate chamber, Calhoun came by, helped by two staff members. He recognized her.

"My child, I am too weak to stop and talk to you."

Then he was escorted to his desk. She remembered those days in Mississippi, when she had first met him. She had been in awe of this famous political figure and could not believe at the time she had attracted the attention of such a powerful man. In her youth she had even fantasized about him. Their exchange of letters had been constant for years and then slowed to a trickle. As she took her seat in the gallery, she saw someone else was reading his speech for him. He was too ill to stand.

Calhoun saw her in the gallery and gave her a look of acknowledgment. His mind raced back to an earlier time when he had met this young woman who was so full of life and energy. She had been like a magnet to him then. After a brief moment, he turned his head back and listened to the words being spoken. He knew this would be his last address to the Senate.

Varina wrote a friend in Natchez, describing her experiences in the capital.

"Washington is such an exciting place. To be at the center of power has been exhilarating. We have had private dinners at the executive mansion with President Taylor on several occasions. Even though the president is a Whig, and Jeff is a Democrat, they are political allies. The president relies heavily on Jeff for advice, and he even told Jeff that he agrees with his position defending Southern rights."

Shortly after Varina left for Mississippi, Calhoun died. The Senate recessed and Jeff was chosen as part of an official delegation to travel to Charleston to attend his funeral. It was April and the azaleas and other flowers were in bloom in the historical city that had once served as South Carolina's capital.

* * *

The crowd was heavy. They filled the entire Citadel Square. From the square the funeral procession moved down Calhoun Street to City Hall. There, the body lay in state for two days while thousands marched by the casket to view this great statesman of the nation. On the morning of the third day, he was buried in the graveyard of Saint Philip's Church.

On the first day after Jeff had arrived by ship, he had unexpectedly heard his name called while strolling down King Street. As he turned, his brain searched for the name attached to that female voice.

"Constance?"

"It's been a long time. I suppose you are here for the funeral."

"I'm part of the Senate delegation.

"I know this is somewhat forward of me, but would you have time for a cup of tea?"

Constance suggested a place nearby. It turned out that she was a widow who lived on Tradd Street with her two children. Jeff found her more beautiful than ever.

During his stay, Jeff spent time with Constance whenever he had an opportunity. She asked him to stay longer after the funeral, and he found an excuse to do so. But he knew his duties lay elsewhere, and he finally had to bid her farewell, much to his regret. In violation of convention, they openly embraced in public at the docks before he boarded the ship that would take him up the eastern seaboard toward Washington. He did not know that Varina had decided, without consulting him, to return to Washington after a short stay at *Brierfield*. When Jeff arrived back at the capital, she questioned him why he had delayed his return. His answers were evasive, and she could never ascertain the reason.

On July 5, President Taylor became ill. His condition rapidly declined. Jeff spent many hours at his bedside, sometimes with Varina at his side. The end came quickly. His last words were to Jeff.

"Apply the Constitution to the measure, Sir, regardless of consequences."

Times were heating up in the Senate, and for the first time Jeff spoke about the danger of disunion if the North did not respect Southern rights. He continued to speak out on the matter, hoping those in Congress from the Northern states would see the danger of grabbing too much power as their influence continued to grow.

"For the first time in the history of this republic, we are in the process of destroying the balance of power between the states."

The South, which had control over the fate of the nation since its foundation, was increasingly being pushed into a minority status. Paranoia began to spread among its people. They feared an increasingly strong central government would emerge that would destroy the independence of their states. They saw state sovereignty as the last defense of their individual and property rights. Increasingly, they looked to the Constitution as their only safeguard. But they knew the Constitution could be changed if the hostile majority became too large. This was their greatest fear.

In April, when Jeff returned to Mississippi, he was surprised by the political fever in the state. His old enemy, Senator Foote, had announced for governor and was running on a platform that included his vote in favor of the 1850 compromise. He had managed to unite under his banner the remnants of the Whig party and a group that took the title of Union Democrats. Planning to oppose him was Jefferson Davis' old friend, General Quitman. He had become a rabid secessionist, who announced his intention to take Mississippi out of the Union. The Democratic regulars became alarmed, as it quickly became apparent that the people of Mississippi were in no mood to leave the union. At political stump meetings throughout the state, crowds heckled Quitman, and many called him a traitor. Soon the powerful men of the party were making pilgrimages to *Brierfield* beseeching Jeff to have his name put before the upcoming convention as a candidate for governor.

"You are the only person who has the strength to stop Quitman from getting the nomination," they said. "His election as governor would be a catastrophe for Mississippi, and the election of Foote would be a disaster for States Rights."

Jeff finally gave his consent to be the Union candidate for the party regulars. Quitman withdrew, and Jeff resigned from the Senate to run for governor.

Varina was puzzled by his action.

"Why in the world have you taken such a course?" she asked. "You have never wanted to be governor. Remember when you turned down the opportunity after the Mexican War."

"I prefer to stay in Washington. But I have a duty to my state. Quitman's radical secessionist views would be a disaster for Mississippi if he were elected. That man might start a war."

"But you will be the Union man in the race for your party's nomination."

"What's wrong with that?"

"You've raised the issue of secession many times on the floor of the Senate."

"Only to make the North aware of what could happen if they overstep certain boundaries in dealing with the Southern states. I'm loyal to our republic. There lies the hope of all the states."

"Your decision has something to do with your intense dislike of Foote," Varina said.

"Perhaps that is a factor."

When Davis accepted the nomination at the party convention, he was not well. But the regulars had promised him they would campaign throughout the state on his behalf. He left Jackson the day after the convention and arrived in *Brierfield* deadly ill with the reoccurring malaria. Varina had him taken from the coach and placed in their bed. His left eye became swollen to the point she thought it might burst. The room had to be kept completely dark. She stayed by his bedside, and during the periods that he was awake, she read to him. Finally the crisis passed. The last three weeks of the campaign, Jeff's health somewhat recovered, and he hit the campaign trail to dispel rumors that he was dead. He was surprised to find most voters agreed with Foote's support of the 1850 Compromise. They did not understand his opposition to it.

"The effect of this act is to treat Southerners as second-class citizens," he said consistently from the stump. "Under it, you will be prohibited from taking your property into all the territories of the United States."

Jeff could not make them understand that the law drew a distinction between the citizens of the various states. When election ballots were counted, Jeff had lost by 999 out of 57,717 vote's casts. The defeat was seen as a victory since Foote had been expected to win by a landslide. From the close vote, it was obvious Jeff was still very popular in Mississippi. If he had not been bedridden during most of the campaign, he would have won the election.

Out of public office for the first time in years, Jeff returned to the life of a planter on the Mississippi. He wrote a letter to his friend, Sidney Johnson.

"I find myself content to spend hours every day working with Varina in the grand flower garden she has designed. In the morning their wonderful scent drifts through the window. We often lie there enjoying a pleasant conversation while waiting for the house servants to bring us coffee and breakfast. Afterwards, she and I ride across our estate, and I show her places that I plan to plant orchards of apples, plums, pears, and peaches. The rest of the day, if I am not involved in one of her projects, is spent with James. I am so blessed to have him at my side. Without his help, *Brierfield* would never have functioned in my absence."

Just when Jeff thought there was nothing that could bring him more happiness than he already enjoyed, Varina had a pleasant surprise for him.

As they lay in bed one evening reading, she turned to Jeff and said in a soft voice, "I'm pregnant."

"How did this happen?" he said without thinking, even as a look of unbelievable happiness spread across his face.

Varina smiled as he pulled her close to him. Moments later, he removed her cotton slip. She felt his heart beat against her naked chest. They made love, and the tenderness he showed her that night made the sex between them even better than usual.

During the months of her pregnancy, Jeff became almost like her servant, waiting on her at every opportunity. She began to grow more mature in her treatment of him, even as her changing hormones made her less understanding in dealing with the house slaves. During this time, she finally began to appreciate the characteristics that made her husband respond to various situations.

She wrote a letter to a friend in Natchez.

"My husband is truly a generous man, but he is somewhat rigid in his idea of how things should work. Slaves, children, and women all respond warmly to him, and he reciprocates as long as everyone conforms to the conventional norms of society. He is the first to defend the rights of those that he perceives are below him, but he does not get along well with his equals, nor with those over him that abuse their authority. While he has a tendency to be authoritarian, he rebels against anyone who shows a similar trait."

Jeff's time at home separated from public discourse ended when his close friend Franklin Pierce of New Hampshire became the Democratic nominee for President. With the Whigs showing renewed strength in Mississippi, he took to the campaign trail again and even spoke on behalf of the ticket as far away as Memphis. But when he learned of the death of James, he hurried home to be at the funeral.

Varina wrote a friend about the occasion.

"The funeral was such a sad event. All the slaves from *Brierfield* were in attendance. The Episcopal minister from Natchez, where James was a member, performed the service. I don't think anyone was more grief stricken than Jeff. When he embraced James' wife and children, he cried like a baby."

On July 30, Jeff and Varina's first child was born. They named him Samuel Emory Davis after his grandfather. The child drove away the deep melancholy that had gripped him after the death of James. Looking toward a future with a family where Varina would be the center, Jeff changed his will by making Varina sole beneficiary of his estate.

For several days slaves appeared at the house to bring gifts for the baby in the form of homespun clothing and food from their gardens. They were allowed to hold and kiss the child. One old slave woman, who was known for her ability to predict the future, told Varina, "this little Massa will never have to work." Words that would later come back to haunt Jeff and Varina.

THE SECRETARY
OF WAR

Varina thought that Jeff's public life was over, and he would remain at her side to run the plantation. It was something that should have had his attention, but because with the death of James there was no one he could depend on to make it prosper. However, everything changed when a message from Pierce arrived after the presidential election. Jeff was offered the position of Secretary of War with the new administration. Varina begged him not to accept. He delayed making a decision for several weeks, but the desire to return to public service proved too great. His acceptance marked the end of his chance to become a wealthy planter. He would henceforth be absent from *Brierfield* for great periods of time. Without James, Jeff would go through many white overseers, constantly firing them for what he perceived was mistreatment of his slaves. Finally, he was forced to put great reliance on Ben Montgomery to keep things going at *Brierfield*. Though

Ben was a brilliant man, he had Joseph's plantation to run, as well as his own enterprises. The plantation would never again receive the attention it needed to become a success.

When Jeff assumed control of the War Department, the U. S. Army had only 10,000 men and officers scattered across thousands of miles of frontier and coastal defenses. Americans feared a large standing army, and was content to rely on state militia volunteers whenever a crisis arose. Since there was no retirement system, many of the officers were old but continued to serve.

Jeff's predecessors in the office had never involved themselves in the everyday operation of the War Department. He was an exception to this mode of operation. He was a workaholic by nature and a micro-manager. No one could ever accuse him of not being diligent in carrying out his duties, when given a task. He immediately immersed himself in even the most mundane matters of the bureaucracy under him, as well as the military itself. Not only was this his nature, but also work assuaged the loneliness he felt being away from his wife and child. He wrote Varina constantly expressing his love and detailing his activities at the department.

Dear Varina,
My heart aches when I think of you and Samuel. Washington can be a very lonely place when the ones you love are so far away. Hopefully in the coming months, I will be able to return to your loving arms, if only for a few weeks.

This month has been unusually hard. Hundreds of office seekers have been knocking on my door demanding employment in the War Office. Although the past policy had been to dismiss employees who were appointed in a prior administration and replace them with the supporters of the new administration, I have refused to do so. Men should be hired on merit, and men should be dismissed only if they do not perform well. This is the standard I shall impose during my term here. I also hope to establish a merit system for the promotion of officers. The present system of promotion on seniority has filled the officer corps with men of high rank who are incompetent. In this regards I have convinced several West Point graduates to return to military duty. One of these is Albert Sidney Johnson who is now Colonel of the Second Cavalry.

Thinking of you always,
Love,
Jeff

Varina could not help but notice the deference she was given at social gathering she attended in Natchez and elsewhere. Many times she was told by acquaintances that Jeff was going to be President of the United States someday. She had begun to believe that might be possible. After all, his name had been mentioned at the last two national conventions. In the meantime while he was away, her days were filled with the responsibilities of being a mother and supervising some of the aspects of *Brierfield*. Her flower garden was being constantly extended as she received new varieties of plants.

During this time she was in constant communication with her friend in Natchez about Jeff's activities in Washington.

"Jeff has grown so important in the eyes of the administration. He has become the president's right hand man on matters beyond the War Department. At least twice a week, they meet over a private dinner at the executive mansion. And now, the president has added to Jeff's burden by putting him in charge of remodeling the House and Senate wings at the Congressional Building. He is enthusiastic as always when architecture is involved. He will make it beautiful, but with an emphasis on comfort. He has been recently studying Roman and Greek designs, and I suspect he will incorporate that into the building making it a showcase for the nation.

"Our home at *Brierfield* has finally been completed. I spent last week in New Orleans purchasing furniture and accessories. Joseph provided me with a line of credit. Some things were quite expensive, I hope Jeff and Joseph will not be displeased.

"On another positive note, Jeff has asked me to come and live in Washington for the duration of his term. I think little Samuel and I shall go, though I worry about leaving our plantation with no master about. I certainly cannot leave until my items from New Orleans arrive."

* * *

Varina and Samuel arrived in Washington and a joyful Jeff met them at the railroad station. After he had given his wife a long embrace, he held the child in his arms and delivered several kisses to the child. Together they rode in a coach to Willard's Hotel. Jeff had been staying there, but now with his family having joined him, they would need a house in the area.

"You can start looking tomorrow," Jeff said.

"This is so exciting," Varina said.

She was different from the young woman who had first accompanied her husband to Washington. She had matured in many ways, and this maturity was heightened by the fact that she was a mother.

A month later they were still living in a hotel.

"I just can't believe how hard it is to find a suitable home near the War Department," she said to Jeff, who was holding Samuel in his arms, while he observed the people below on the street.

"When I was at the executive mansion today, I mentioned our problem," Jeff said. "The president has a friend that might be interested in renting us a place. Hopefully, I'll hear back from him on that matter in the coming days."

They found a house on Fourteenth Street within easy walking distance of the War Department. Jeff found himself leaving work early on many days, anxious to spend time with "Le man", as he called him. The child would wait by the door in the evenings in anticipation of his father walking through it. Jeff, unlike his own father, never hesitated to show his son demonstrative love.

Jeff and Varina became an intimate part of the new administration when the couple were drawn into a close relationship with Franklin and his wife, Jane. After the first New Year's Day reception at the executive mansion, Jane spent the rest of her husband's term upstairs in her room writing letters to her deceased son, Bennie. The boy had been killed in a train accident when the coach he was traveling in with his parents broke loose from the train and rolled down an embankment two months before Franklin was sworn in as president. He had been their last remaining child.

"Jeff," the President said one day when the two were alone in his study, "I need Varina's help. Jane has become so melancholy, she refuses to leave her room."

"The death of a son would certainly cause any mother to grieve," Jeff said.

"But I don't think she will ever get over it," the President said. "She blames me for his death. Jane believes it is God's punishment because of my political ambitions. When I wanted to run for president, she resisted it. I convinced her that living in Washington would be good for Bennie. Now our marriage is doomed to be a hollow one."

"I will discuss this matter with Varina," Jeff said. "I'm sure she would be willing to substitute for Jane as a hostess at the executive mansion. Perhaps she could spend time with your wife. Female companionship may help Jane, though no parent will ever get over the loss of a child. As your close friend, I have seen what suffering you have had to endure."

When Jeff breeched the subject with Varina, she accepted the responsibility, and for the rest of the Pierce administration, she acted as the First Lady at social function in the executive mansion.

All seemed well in Jeff's world. He held a position in the Cabinet, his relationship with his wife had reached new heights as they learned to respect one another, and he had a child that he adored. Then tragedy struck.

"I think he has the measles," Varina said one morning.

"I'm going to get a doctor now," Jeff said.

"Aren't you going to work?"

"Not until I know that LE Man is all right."

Jeff did not go to work and when word came of urgent matters that needed to be attended to, he did not respond. Samuel, who was less than two years old, passed away one night while Jeff and Varina sat beside his bed and cried. The prophecy of the old slave at *Brierfield* upon the child's birth had been fulfilled. The little Massa would never have to work.

The grief brought Jeff and Varina closer together. And for the first time in their marriage, Varina was the strong one, who had to try to console a man who would not be consoled, but wept like a child for several days. Samuel's death brought Pierce and Jeff even closer, for the president had lost a child, and he knew what it was to have unbearable grief.

The house contained too much sadness so they moved to a home on Thirteenth Street. There the depression was lifted by news that Varina was pregnant again. On February 25 1855, a daughter, Margaret Howell, was born. With his time in the Cabinet almost concluded, Jeff took a few weeks off from his duties at the War Department, and Varina and he spent weeks vacationing in New Hampshire. Upon his return, he traveled for the first time through the South by railroad on the trip back to Mississippi. Many in his political circle saw him as a possible candidate for president if Pierce did not seek a second term.

When he returned to Washington, Jeff was not in a happy mood, for he had left Varina and his new child in Mississippi, and he desperately missed them. His personal misery showed in his temperament. He became embroiled in an argument with Robert Toombs of Georgia, and when he believed the man called him dishonest, he challenged him to a duel. When the matter was resolved, he once again thought someone had impugned his honor, and he called out the culprit, Judah Benjamin of Louisiana to a duel. He quickly realized that he was in error and withdrew the challenge after issuing one of his rare apologies.

At the National Democratic Convention that year, Pierce stood for reelection, and Jeff remained true to his friend. Even when it was becoming increasingly apparent that the party would not nominate Pierce for a second term, Jeff refused to allow his name to be submitted to the convention. "I could not do such a dishonorable thing," he said to delegates who came to him from various sections of the country. He encouraged anyone who would listen, that if Pierce didn't have the votes, they should give the vote to a Northern Democrat.

"The settlement of the slavery issued can best be accomplished by a Yankee, for it will help us with our allies outside the South."

Jeff was not upset when James Buchannan of Pennsylvania was elected as the nominee and subsequently went on to win the Presidency. Though he could have remained at the War Department, he chose to return to Mississippi. This was in some part due to his bad health, and Varina's own health problems, following complications she suffered in giving birth to another child, which they named Jefferson Davis Jr. Before leaving, they sold everything they had collected during their stay in Washington, which included horses, a carriage, curtains, and china.

"My time as a public servant is over," he said to a close friend. "I must look to my home at *Brierfield* and to the crops. Both of which have suffered in my absence."

The trip was not a pleasant one. The children developed chicken pox. Jeff and Varina had to take care of them on various modes of transportation as they struggled to reach their sanctuary. Unlike other trips, the conversation around him this time was centered on the fate of the union. Jeff had not realized that while he was isolated in the capital, the political discussion had changed. Many were giving serious thought to the possibility that the union might dissolve, and now rarely was the word "traitor" used against those who advocated secession.

THE STATESMAN

If Varina thought the weeks that Jeff spent at *Brierfield* would last, she was to be sadly disappointed. They were home only a few months when the powerful political factions in Mississippi united behind Jeff to fill a Senate seat. Varina, whose health had returned, for the first time did not object. She hoped to join him soon in the capital. In the short time since her return to Mississippi, she realized how much she missed living at the center of power.

Jeff entered his duties in the Senate with the same determination he had always exhibited when he held public office, but the Senate he returned to was a different body than the one in which he previously served. It seemed that the great men like Calhoun, Clay, and Webster had been replaced with lesser men who were incapable of preserving the union.

In a letter to a friend he wrote, "I hate disunionist, but I believe a state has a right to secede." Only in his own mind could he reconcile those two inconsistent thoughts and not see a conflict. Even his friend, when reading the letter, was confused by the statement.

Jeff had friends on all sides of the political spectrum. Even when someone disagreed with him, they admired the logical way in which he delivered his argument. He did become testy at times, but his mood seemed to lighten after Varina arrived in Washington with the children. Securing a house, they settled in, and Jeff's world was again focused on more than the debates in the Senate.

In February, Jeff became critically ill. It started with laryngitis, which somehow led to an infection once again in his left eye. His condition deteriorated so rapidly that the doctor thought he might not recover. For a period of seven weeks he lay in a darkened room unable to see out of his left eye, and was barely able to speak. On many occasions he refused to eat.

"I'm in too much anguish."

Senator William Seward, a close personal friend, frequently came by and sat with him so Varina could get some rest. After being away from the Senate chamber for many weeks, the Senators looked up one day to see the Calhoun of Mississippi return to his desk. He looked weak and pale, but he was back.

Jeff was blessed that the Senate adjournment came early in July. Leaving Washington, he took his family to New England where they stayed for four months. Both Jeff and Varina would remember this as one of the most wonderful times in their marriage. On many occasions, he was asked to speak about the state of the union. He spoke in her defense in such a manner that when he later returned to Mississippi, he discovered that the secessionists who now held the power in his state were greatly displeased with him. The effect of his speeches in the North spread dissent beyond the borders of Mississippi. Fire-eaters throughout the South denounced him. It took substantial efforts for him to mend his political bridges. For the first time, he began to feel that a day of reckoning was coming, and there was nothing he could do to save the old union of states.

Returning to Washington when the Senate went into session in January, he was caught on the horns of a political dilemma. Should he pursue the presidency and find the middle ground as many encouraged him to do, or remain the spokesman for only one section of his country. He had been received warmly during his stay in New England, where his reputation in the Mexican War had made him a national hero second only to Taylor. He also had made several visits to New York and Pennsylvania where he spoke to large crowds. In a national campaign, he could remind the voters of the North that his family line sprang from Philadelphia, and that Varina's grandfather had been governor of New Jersey. And in the frontier states, he could emphasis how he had help defend the West as an Indian fighter.

In his first speech upon his return to the Senate, Jeff sought to appeal to all sections of the country. The time in the North had given him hope that the union could be saved.

"True men can affect much by giving to the opposite section, respect for the views held by others. My recent trip has shown me that our differences are less than I suppose. The men of this Congress must put aside pettiness and their increasing lack of civility toward one another and focus on saving the union."

Only a short time after his return to the Senate, his mood began to shift again. He could not resist rising to the defense of the South when she was attacked. While his view of the Constitution was one that still had many adherents in the North and West, the issue of slavery had now so muddied the water, that the diverse sections of the country were no longer listening to the actual words spoken, but read other motives into them.

The session of Congress was short. It recessed on March 3. Jeff returned to *Brierfield*, leaving Varina in Washington for she was too far along in her pregnancy to travel. There was much work to do. The last two years, the cotton crop had been destroyed by flooding from the Mississippi. Jeff had to draw on his savings from the prosperity of previous years to take care of his slaves whom he considered his responsibility as members of his family circle. He went to work, repairing damaged dikes, rebuilding sheds, and replanting Varina's garden, which had been destroyed. A few weeks after he arrived at the plantation, word reached him that Varina had a baby boy. Unlike her other births, which had left her in poor health for weeks afterward, she had come through this ordeal without any problems.

Varina had been so pleased with her husband. The past term in Washington had been a pleasant experience, and Jeff had remained in good health during the session. They had been able for the first time to attend the numerous social functions. There, Jeff was the life of the party, dancing, joking and telling of his experiences on the frontier and in Mexico, but now an event occurred that unsettled the domestic peace. A dark cloud once again hovered over their marriage.

"We have a beautiful baby boy," she wrote Jeff. "He is healthy and so am I. His features remind me so much of my father that I would dearly love to name the child after him. However, I shall abide by your wishes and name him after Joseph, though you know it gives me no pleasure to do so."

In another letter to a friend in Vicksburg she expressed similar feelings.

"The news that I should have no input into the name of my child has so depressed me that I have taken to my bed. The doctor says that I am running a fever. The servants have complete care of my children, for I do not have the strength to take care of them."

While Jeff was at *Brierfield*, there was another flood. The water rose so high that Jeff could step from his porch into a boat. Most of the hard work replacing Varina's garden had been wasted.

Varina upon receiving a correspondence from him, communicated the news about the damage in a letter to Jane Pierce in New Hampshire.

"I have never known Jeff so distressed," she wrote. "A levee upstream broke, and the wave of water drowned much of the livestock. Many cotton fields suffered flood damage, so there will be no crop this year. All the work he spent replanting my gardens has turned out to have been a waste of time. He must start over again."

From a friend in Washington, Jeff received a telegram informing him that his wife was ill. Alarmed, he dropped everything and left for Washington immediately, leaving Montgomery in charge of *Brierfield*. When Jeff arrived, he hired a coach at the railroad station and went directly to see Varina.

"Why didn't you send word of your illness?"

"I couldn't bear to place another burden upon your shoulders."

"You are the most important thing in the world to me. I could not bear losing you."

"I love you Jeff, but you were wrong to insist that I name the child after your brother."

Jeff chose to ignore her comment. He took her in his arms and held her for a long time.

After his return, Varina quickly regained her health as her harsh feelings against him moderated.

Jeff suffered a recurrence of an infection in his eye after his return to the capital. A surgeon operated on it and drained fluid that had built up in the cornea. After recuperating, he took his family to Maryland for a vacation during the month of June before returning to *Brierfield*. He left his family in Washington because it was the fever season in Mississippi. While in his home state, he attended the Democratic Convention. Many delegates wanted to put his name forward to head the national ticket. He refused to consider it, and instead he encouraged them to support a Northern Democrat who would protect Southern rights. Despite his objection, the majority of the Mississippi delegation voted to support him at the National Convention that was to be held at Charleston in April.

"Joseph," he said to his brother when they were alone, "with the disintegration of the Whig party, there is great danger that this new

Republican Party will win the next election. It is not a national party, but a sectional one. It can win without the support of any electoral votes from the thirteen Southern states. We must have a candidate from the North as our nominee. Otherwise, we are doomed."

"Do you have someone in mind?"

"Franklin Pierce. He has nationwide recognition having already served as president, and he could carry Pennsylvania and New England."

"You should write him."

Jeff wrote a letter and posted it before he left Jackson.

Back in the capital, Jeff and many other Southern congressmen were upset that the Charleston meeting had failed to nominate a candidate, and that Alabama, Arkansas, Georgia, Louisiana, Mississippi, South Carolina, and Texas had walked out of the convention. Jeff prepared a letter encouraging them to return to the party and participate in the National Convention that was to reconvene in Baltimore on June 15th. He asked eighteen other southern congressmen to sign the letter, and he sent it to the state delegations that had bolted. As a result, many of these delegates came to Baltimore, but Stephen Douglas, seeing that their admittance would jeopardize his nomination, had them refused entrance. As a result of Douglas' action, Virginia, California, Oregon, and several delegates from Kentucky and Massachusetts walked out. The remaining delegates nominated Douglas. The Democratic Party was now shattered.

A week later, Jeff wrote his brother, Joseph.

"I still retain hope that the Republicans can be defeated and the country saved. The delegates that had bolted from the party met and nominated John Breckinridge as their candidate for president. I had Breckinridge over for dinner last night. The man professed he had not wanted the nomination and intended to withdraw. He is a man much to be admired, having served in the House and as Vice President before coming to the Senate this year. He would make a fine president, but is shrewd enough to know that a campaign by him would only result in helping the enemies of the South. When he told me of his plans to withdraw, I persuaded him to delay until I have time to consult with Douglas. I also met with Bell who is the candidate of the Constitutional Party. He, like Breckinridge, agreed to withdraw, if Douglas would step aside so that a new Democratic convention could be called, where a viable candidate could be chosen to face the Republicans in November.

"If the Senator from Illinois can be convinced that with Breckinridge and Bell in the race, he stands no chance of election, then perhaps, he will withdraw for the good of the party and most importantly for the good of our nation. Though Douglas and I are not on the best of terms, I am willing to humble myself by begging him to meet with me about this matter. There is no honor in letting my pride stand in the way when the survival of the union is at stake."

Joseph received another correspondence from Jeff two weeks later.

"I must tell you that Douglas agreed to meet. But when we were together there was nothing I could do to convince him to put patriotism first. He said the nomination was his, and he will not relinquish.

"If there is war, Stephen Douglas must share much of the blame. He is the one who destroyed the Missouri Compromise. His handiwork in that regards was his ambitious plan to prevent the transcontinental railroad from taking a southern route. I had convinced Franklin Pierce to pay Mexico five million dollars for the Gadsden Purchase, which gave us Arizona and New Mexico, a necessary purchase for the southern transcontinental route to California. But he was determined that the railroad line pass through his region to California. To accomplish this he needed to bring those areas into statehood. To get northern support, he pushed popular sovereignty. The direct result of his politics was bloody Kansas and that led to John Brown's raid. Now the Union is in danger of becoming divided.

"Our only other hope lay in my good friend, William Steward, winning the Republican nomination. But alas, the radical Abraham Lincoln prevailed. I fear we must prepare to go our own way and form a confederation of Southern states. Hopefully, if this unfortunate event occurs, the North will let us go in peace. There is strong sentiment in the North that force should not be used to preserve our compact of states. Having access to many Northern papers in Washington, it appears that Lincoln is hell-bent to occupy the South, regardless of the blood that will be spilled, and there is terrible political pressure on him not to moderate the views he spoke of in his campaign.

"The events at Harper's Ferry by the fanatic John Brown have unduly terrified the South. They believe that the North plans to arm our slaves to rise up and slaughter us. This is nonsense. I do not fear my people at *Brierfield*, for they are like family to me. If troublemakers were to descend upon us, I have faith that they would stand shoulder to shoulder beside me to repel the invaders. If the facts in Virginia were closely examined, the public would see that is exactly what happened there."

* * *

The election of Lincoln, who had run a sectional campaign and secured the majority of electoral votes, though he obtained less than thirty-nine percent of the popular vote, sent the Southern cotton states into a panic. The Mississippi governor wrote Jeff the week after the election and indicated he planned to call the Legislature into session to consider secession. He asks Jeff to return home and lead the efforts of the fire-eaters. Jeff declined.

"As you must be aware, I have not been a member of those groups that are anxious to separate their states from this union. In fact, I have frequently opposed the disunionist. This does not mean that I will not support my state whatever path she may proceed down. My first loyalty is to Mississippi, as I believe that every citizen should be loyal to their state and through their state to the union.

"Although I have delivered many speeches in Mississippi where my words declared that our state should prepare to secede immediately if Lincoln was elected, I now have reservations about such actions. As we approach the abyss, it might be better to wait and see what actions the new administration will take before decisions are made that could bring on a war between the states."

* * *

During the first forty-five days of the session, Jeff worked diligently with others in the congress to prevent the rupture of the union. But when a close friend put him in possession of documents that revealed Lincoln's intentions to force through an appropriation bill for a large army to occupy any state that had seceded or indicated a movement in that direction, he knew the time for delay and compromise had passed. There was to be no more vacillating. He sent his governor a letter informing him of Lincoln's intent.

"You must act now, for federal forces will move quickly after Lincoln's inauguration on March 4th. The states who intend to secede should, with all deliberate speed, form a confederation and arm themselves. There will be war, and the amount of blood that will be shed will make both sides wish that reason had prevailed. I shall remain in Washington until Mississippi crosses the Rubicon. After which, I shall have no option but to resign."

South Carolina seceded on December 20th 1860, and was followed by Mississippi on January 9, Florida on January 10, and Alabama on January 11, Georgia on January 19th. Jeff met with the congressional delegation from those states. They decided to resign and called upon their respective states to meet in Montgomery for the purpose of forming a new government. Afterwards, Jeff sent a telegram to Governor John Jones Pettus.

"Judge what Mississippi requires of me and place me accordingly."

Immediately after he sent the telegram, Jeff became deadly ill, and he was confined to his bed. When Senator Steward visited him, Jeff disclosed to him information that had come to him through a friend.

"There is a plot, by some irresponsible radical hot bloods in Maryland, to kidnap Lincoln before his inauguration. I was asked to pass this information to someone close to him. Lawlessness is something I cannot condone."

When Steward left Jeff's bedside, he carried with him all the details of the plot.

Varina wrote to Jane Franklin.

"Jeff has been so ill. I believe it is caused by the stress he feels about the breakup of the union. Yesterday several fire-eaters from Alabama visited. Their excitement about the separation of the states left him extremely distraught."

On January 19th, Jeff received word from the governor that he should return home immediately. As he prepared for departure, he penned a letter to his friend, Franklin Pierce.

"I am on the eve of taking my final leave from the federal government. There is great doubt in my mind that the separation of the states will come about peacefully, but if we cannot go peacefully, the sword will have to resolve the matter. I do not shrink from this, though a civil war has only horror for me.

"The first possible collision may come at Charleston. Governor Pickens has asked my military advice about Fort Sumter. The cadets at the Citadel under the command of Major Stevens have already fired on a re-supply ship, *The Star of the West*. I advised him not to attack the fort until his military forces are strong enough to do so. Robert Anderson is in command, and he will fight if he is attacked. The best solution would be to let the fort run out of food and water so that his surrender will be with honor. If at all possible, the South must not fire the first shot and enrage the patriots in the North. This would destroy the support of those who would let us go peacefully, despite Lincoln's determination that there shall be war."

* * *

Varina watched from the Senate gallery. It was a sad moment. Her husband had struggled to get out of bed where he had lain ill for several days. He was so weak that she had dressed him. Now pale and emaciated, he rose from his desk to give his final address to the Senate. The gallery was full of spectators. The seats in the chambers were filled except those few that sadly lay empty because their members had already departed to go home to their seceding states.

Jeff looked at the body he was about to address. Many memories passed through his mind, and as he began to speak he had to struggle to keep his emotions under control.

"I rise to inform this body that my membership in this August body is ended. Despite our many disagreements over the years, I want to assure you that I leave this glorious chamber with no personal ill feeling toward anyone, whatever words may have passed between us in the heat of debate. In the presence of God, I wish you well. Whatever offense that has been done to me, I forgive, and for any offense I have given, I apologize. It has been an honor to have known you and to have grappled together with the many issues that have faced our republic. I regret our parting, but events have now overtaken me, and it now only remains for me to bid you a final adieu."

Varina was surprised by the reaction. The gallery and the chamber erupted in applause. Senators gathered around Jeff and said their good-byes. She noticed many had tears in their eyes. Tears were being shed for him and for the nation.

That night she awoke to find him on his knees beside the bed praying. In the darkness she heard him say, "May God have us in His holy keeping, and grant that before it is too late peaceful counsel may prevail." This was the first time she had seen him turn to God in a crisis. Soon he rejoined her in the bed. As she held him tight like you would a child, her face was dampened by his tears. The next morning they left for Mississippi.

When Jeff and his family arrived in Jackson, he was met by the governor and a state delegation. It was there Jeff learned that he had been appointed a commander of the state militia. His plans to return to *Brierfield* were delayed for several days while he organized the bureaucracy of the new army. He soon discovered there was a shortage of arms.

"We shall need more firearms, ammunition, and cannon, Governor."

"I think you overestimate the danger."

"We must prepare, prepare, prepare. And may God help us, for war is a dreadful calamity, even when it is made against strangers, and it will be more so because it will be against our fellow Americans."

Jeff could not understand the failure of the leaders in the cotton states to comprehend the danger facing them from an enemy that had overwhelming resources in materials and men. As the former Secretary of War, he knew where the munitions plants, manufactures of cannons and other armaments were located. They were in the Northern states. The United States Navy would remain loyal to Washington, and the South had no fleet. The best and most numerous railroads were not located in the south. This would deprive the cotton states of the ability to transport troops to the field of battle. The North would suffer no such problem.

* * *

"We have finally reached *Brierfield*," Varina wrote Jane Pierce, a person whose friendship had become extremely important after they shared the grief of losing a child. "The place is in need of supervision, and I hope Jeff will rest his mind by taking to task the labor that must be done to get the fields in order. It will do him good to so occupy his mind, for his thoughts are now on the crisis at hand. He can't seem to stop talking to others about the catastrophe ahead, and at the same time in private conversation with Joseph and me, he expresses hope that somehow the North will guarantee our equal rights, and the country will be re-united."

Jeff stayed busy with the work at hand. His slaves seemed happy to have him, Varina, and the children home again. Varina and he spent many hours repairing the damages to her garden that had suffered neglect while they were away. Once again, Jeff was able to spend time in the evening with Joseph, sitting in the extensive library where they discussed the disturbing crisis.

"The fire-eaters have brought us to this point. I'm glad you did not embrace their cause until no other option existed," Joseph said.

"There is no turning back," Jeff said. "I had hoped they would let us go in peace, but now Lincoln has resolved that the issue will be decided by the force of arms. He is determined to force us back into the Union. Democracy upon the point of a bayonet, how strange a concept."

"I don't disagree that this union is made up of a compact of the states, and that a state should not be forced to remain against its will," Joseph said. "But this issue of slavery has muddled the whole concept of State's Rights. Slavery is a dying institution. Most of the major European countries have abolished it in their empires. I know you may disagree, but I wish we could free our slaves. Many Southerners would if they could figure a way to do it without threatening the social structure. We are already moving in that direction, anyway. The master-slave relationship is evolving into a master-servant one, and from that it will gradually evolve even further."

'I don't disagree. Slaves will eventually be freed by the individual states, even without federal intervention. Slavery is not the real issue. It is the relationship of the states to the national government. No one is going to fight and die on the battlefield to preserve slavery."

"Do you expect an office in the new government that is being formed in Montgomery by the states that have seceded?"

"I'm old and in poor health. I'd like simply to stay at *Brierfield* and spend the rest of my life there with my family undisturbed."

"In other words, you are like the South, you just want to be left alone."

* * *

When Jeff received word from the governor to join him on a trip to Montgomery, he chose to ignore it. He remained isolated on his plantation and made no attempt to have any contact with the new government being formed. He did not desire a position, but in his heart he expected to be called upon to be its Commander-in-Chief. Though he hoped this would not be conferred upon him.

The morning of February 10, Jeff and Varina were working in her garden when a rider approached. As he drew close, the excitement on his face and the sweat dripping from his horse showed that the telegram in his hand was important. Jeff read it over several times before turning to Varina and sharing its content.

"They have elected me the Provisional President of the Confederacy."

She saw from his facial expression that the surprise appointment brought him no joy. But she knew he would accept the responsibility because of his rigid concept of public duty. He had never failed to respond to the call of his people, and this time would be no exception.

When the rider departed, he carried with him a written response to the government at Montgomery. Jeff had accepted the post of Provisional President of the seven states that had formed a new nation. Soon the number of states in the Confederacy would number eleven, and if it had not been for the use of force by Washington, it would have numbered thirteen.

The next day Jeff said farewell to Varina and his children. Outside, the slaves gathered. He gave a short speech from the front porch, and then went among them and spoke to them individually expressing his affection for them.

Time slipped away and Jeff had to rush when he heard the steamer signaling its arrival at Davis Bend. Ben Montgomery and several blacks rowed him down a small stream until they reached the river, but before they could reach the dock at Davis Bend, the steamer's departing whistle blew. Jeff had them row to the middle of the river and wait for the ship to appear. When the *Natchez* came around the bend, Jeff hailed it and was taken aboard. Montgomery would never see him again.

When he reached Vicksburg he was met by marching military units, one of them carried the tattered flag of the Mississippi Rifles. On Feburary12[th], he reached Jackson. There he spoke before a large crowd that included his brother, Joseph, who would travel to Montgomery with him.

Jeff received word from the delegates at the capital to make haste, and so he departed by train the next day. Along the way crowds gathered to see their new president. Every time the locomotive made a stop, he gave a speech to the cheering crowds. By the time he reached the capital, he had given over thirty speeches and had developed a touch of laryngitis.

By Sunday February 17th, when the train reached Montgomery, Jeff was exhausted. He needed to work on his speech and get some rest for the inauguration the next day. However, at the hotel where he was staying, there was a line of important visitors waiting to speak with him. It was midnight before he had an opportunity to commence writing his thoughts on what he would say in his address to citizens of the new republic.

THE INAUGURATION

The houses of the city were decked out with patriotic banners. A large crowd gathered to observe the swearing in of their new president at the Alabama statehouse, which would also serve as the Confederate capital. Marching down the street were the Columbus Guards dressed in red jackets and blue trouser. Behind the militia was a carriage pulled by six white horses. Inside sat the newly elected President of The Confederate States of America, Jefferson Davis.

As Jeff stepped down from the carriage, the sound of a new tune gaining popularity was played. Many in the crowd caught up in the moment joined in singing "Dixie"; a song that would become the unofficial national anthem of the Confederacy.

Many thoughts were going through Jeff's mind as his introduction was made by Howell Cobb, a former speaker of the United States House of Representative. He wished Varina and the children were there. But he was not alone, for he had seen Joseph in the audience; a man that was more like a father than an older brother. He had guided him in his career and helped form his views of the constitution. Now many of those ideas would be emphasized in this new country where state sovereignty would be held in high regard as it once was in the old union.

The position of President was not one Jeff had sought or desired. It had been thrust upon him. Now he must do his duty to see that the republic prevailed, regardless of the costs in blood. He sensed this attempt to form a new republic might be crushed by the power of the federal government in Washington.

Jeff stepped forward to take the oath. He placed his left hand upon his mother's bible and raised his right hand.

"I, Jefferson Davis, do solemnly swear, that I will faithfully execute the office of Provisional President of The Confederate States of America, and will, to the best of my ability, preserve, protect, and defend the constitution thereof."

At the end of the oath, Jeff turned to the crowd and said, "So Help Me God."

Now as the Provisional Leader, he stepped to the podium and delivered a speech to the people.

"Called to this difficult and responsible station as President of the Provisional Government, which you have instituted, I approach the discharge of the duties assigned to me with humble distrust of my abilities, but with a sustaining confidence in the wisdom of those who are to guide and aide me in the administration of public affairs, and with an abiding faith in the virtue and patriotism of the people."

As the crowd listened in silence, he outlined the basis for the right of states to leave the Union.

"An appeal to the ballot box declared that so far as they were concerned, the government created by the compact should cease to exist. In this they merely asserted a right that the Declaration of Independence defined as inalienable. Of the time and occasion for its exercise, they, as sovereign, were the final judges, each State for itself. The impartial and enlightened verdict of mankind will vindicate their conduct, and He who knows the hearts of men will judge the sincerity with which they have labored to preserve the government of their forefathers, in its spirit and in those rights within it, which were solemnly proclaimed at the birth of the States. When the States entered the Union, it was with the undeniable recognition of the power of the people to resume the authority delegated for the purposes of that government, whenever in their opinion its functions were perverted and its ends defeated. Now by virtue of this authority, time, and occasion, requiring them to exercise it having arrived, the sovereign States here represented have seceded from the Union, and it is a gross abuse of language to denominate the act as rebellion or revolution. They have formed a new alliance, but in each state the government has remained as before. The rights of persons and property have not been disturbed."

Jeff's words perfectly outline the belief of the people in the region. They felt that the compact of states that formed the union was voluntary and that any state could choose to leave.

EPILOGUE

The Civil War was a catastrophe for Jefferson Davis and the South. By the end of the war, he had lost everything and was imprisoned on a charge of treason. The federal government did not pursue those charges after he was released on bail. Ultimately, Jeff and Varina returned to Mississippi where they struggled to start a new life.

FUTURE NOVELS IN THIS SERIES

The second book in this series, Jefferson Davis: The Conflict and Aftermath, is projected to be published in October 2015. The author's present project is Lincoln: Before the Conflict. He plans to finish this manuscript by January 2015.

ACKNOWLEDGMENTS

My friends, Bill Craine, Cheryl Gause, Jane Moon, Stacey Rabon and Sam Rion comments and suggestion along with those of my brother, Waldo, and my son, David, were invaluable in improving the final draft of this novel. Credit must also go to my son, Robert. Without his constant help resolving computer problem, this manuscript would never have been produced.

THE AUTHOR

David Maring is a retired circuit judge who lives in the historic port of Georgetown located on the South Carolina coast. He had ancestors who fought on opposing sides during the War Between The States. His mother's family fought for Southern independence in various South Carolina regiments while his father's people served with regiments from the State of New York that fought to preserve the Union.

Visit the author's website at **www.dmaring.com** to learn more about his other novels that have received recognition in international competition.

The Serpent's Seed -- This is the first thriller in a trilogy about international intrigue. In the underground library at Timbuktu, Professor William Weston discovers a map describing the location of an ancient city located in Iran. He does not realize his excavation will be interrupted by a confrontation between America and Iran, nor does he foresee that he will be drawn into a whirlpool of intrigue that could lead to a nuclear Armageddon.

The Mullahs -- The second book in the trilogy is centered on the original manuscript of the Book of Revelation buried with the Apostle John. During his excavation of the tomb, Weston is confronted with a geopolitical crisis involving Islamic terrorism.

Carolina Justice -- This novel follows the tradition of literature centered around great stories involving racial conflict where the setting is in the segregated South.

Winyah Bay -- This story traces the lives of the inhabitants from the first human footprints upon the shores of the bay. Unforgettable characters are revealed in a mixture of history and romance.